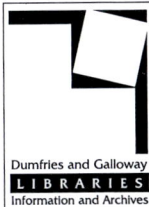

THE DARKNESS WITHIN

THE DARKNESS WITHIN

Sam Stone

CHIVERS

British Library Cataloguing in Publication Data available

This Large Print edition published by AudioGO Ltd, Bath, 2013.
Published by arrangement with the Author

U.K. Hardcover   ISBN   978 1 4713 5914 9
U.K. Softcover   ISBN   978 1 4713 5915 6

Printed and bound in Great Britain by TJ International Limited

1

Teething Troubles

Madison Whitehawk placed her cards down on the table revealing a full house, then reached forward and began to collect the contents of the now-filled poker pot.

'Not so fast,' said Dave Priddy, one of the engineers.

'What?' asked Madison.

'I think you cheated,' Priddy sulked.

'Shut it Priddy, you always think that every time I win,' Madison said, tucking a strand of her dark hair back behind her ear. Her intense blue eyes were serious.

Madison was generally patient with the fiery Irishman but the ship's com system was humming and Priddy, so far, had been unable to fix it. Madison was tired of the complaints from the Bridge about the recurring issues— all of them petty. The way she saw it, the few teething troubles on board weren't much to worry about. It was engine failure that concerned her the most. Fortunately all was running well on board the colony ship *Freedom*. These were just minor niggles.

Freedom was Earth's second Ark and was taking life to the new world while the old one was left behind to die. Madison knew and understood the biblical reference, even though Christianity wasn't her faith. But the natural death of Earth wouldn't be a flood. One day, in the not too distant future, Earth's light would be snuffed out. The cold and barren shell that would remain in orbit around the darkened Sun would be a dead planet. There would be no water, no plant life and certainly no breathable air, much the same as the other rocks that circled the Sun in this solar system.

Scientists had long realised that each of these planets had held life of some sort at one time or another, only to die eventually. Earth of course had been different. It could have lived longer, but humanity had played a heavy part in destroying it. Despite the good intentions that had begun in the twenty-first century, those plans and committees and decisions had sadly been too little too late.

Now the occupants of *Freedom* had many years of space travel ahead of them. Madison felt herself privileged to have made it onto the second colony ship bound for New Earth. The first one, *Adventure*, had successfully reached its destination and so the second wave was now following. More ships would pursue in rapid succession—six months apart, instead of the initial seven years, now that they knew exactly what they were facing.

'She lost the game last night,' Doctor Hallow said as Madison poured her winnings into her rucksack.

Yes. She had lost last night. Quite dramatically. The complication that had occurred with Simon Crichton, the second mate, was something she might have to deal with for the next few years.

Madison recalled how the combination of brandy and synthetic weed had mellowed her reflexes. Otherwise she would never have lost a game of strip poker.

It had been obvious that Crichton had liked what he had seen under her baggy engineer's uniform. And so had the few men that had been up that late watching or participating in the game—Doctor Hallow being one of them.

'Yeah? Who against, Doc?' asked Priddy who fortunately hadn't been around when Madison had quit rather than take off her vest and pants: a mistake that would probably take this whole trip and beyond for her to live down. Now they knew she wasn't quite as tough as she made out.

'Crichton,' said Hallow.

'Shut it, Doc,' Madison scowled.

'Whoa. What happened then?' Priddy asked.

'Nothing,' said Madison.

'She had no credits, so Crichton made her strip,' Mike Gill said. He was wearing a smirk that Madison wanted to wipe right off his face.

'Damn,' said Priddy. 'Wish I'd stayed around to see that!'

Madison stood up. She tried to hide the

3

flush that rushed to her face as she reined in the anger and the unfamiliar feeling of humiliation that she didn't quite know how to deal with. She tried not to notice that all of the men present were watching her closely, maybe even imagining what they had missed when she removed her boiler suit.

'You didn't miss much,' Madison said, making the joke before one of them could.

'I dunno. It was quite a show,' Gill said.

Madison scowled at him.

'Break's over,' she said. 'We've got that com system to fix and you'd better keep your mind on the job this time Priddy, 'cos the Captain was pretty pissed last time he messaged down about it. The constant buzz is upsetting the colonists.'

'Yeah. We can't have *them* upset,' said Hallow. 'What with their fancy sensibilities an' all.'

Madison was a little taken aback to hear the bitterness in the Doctor's voice. It didn't surprise her that the doctor resented the choice of colonists though. True, they all knew that they were chosen for their pure DNA, their intelligence and their ability to breed— just as the crew themselves had. These were all qualities that had rapidly become a rare thing in their generation. Madison and the crew were also privileged. They were, after all, some of the first to be chosen for the journey to New Earth. However, the crew were not as revered

4

as the colonists, most of whom all came from families of wealth and station. Despite the fact that they were all virtually in the same position, the colonists were pampered, while the crew worked. Once on New Earth, however, they would all stay and make a new life on the planet. The colonists would then have to earn their hierarchy by populating the new world with children. They would also be expected to work as hard as everyone else did.

Madison had already passed the fertility tests, though she wasn't keen on the policy of being paired with a 'suitable' partner for breeding when they arrived. That is, unless she paired with someone before then. It wasn't her idea of the future. But once on the colony she hoped to find work—engineers were always needed and since she would have this trip as Chief Engineer to add to her resumé, she knew that her contribution to the building of the new world would be welcome.

The com system buzzed loudly and Hallow, who was standing closest to the speaker, covered his ears.

'Jesus, Priddy. You really need to *fix* that.'

Priddy pushed back his chair from the small table and picked up his toolbox. Madison nodded to him.

'Enough is enough,' she said.

Priddy scurried off as did the rest of the men and women in engineering. But as Madison stowed her bag in her locker she realised that Hallow was still there.

'Why you down here, Doc? I mean you could be in the Officers' Mess drinking the finest wines and brandies and hobnobbing with the colonists?'

'Have you actually spent any time in the company of Captain Fence?' said Hallow.

'Not much. He's usually just barking orders at me.'

'Well, Madison. You're lucky. He's the most boring man I've ever met. And as for the colonists . . . every time I see any of them, it's whines and ailments. Not much there for me to socialise with.'

'Yeah. I guess I hadn't seen it that way,' Madison said.

*   *   *

First Officer Simon Crichton watched the now-tiny Earth slowly receding from the monitor on his desk. They had left Earth's atmosphere, then orbited around the planet for a week to allow the occupants to acclimatise to the ship's gravity field. The gravity generator felt different to the natural gravity of Earth and so the colonists had to learn to move around before the ship could set off on its course towards New Earth.

Though this was a necessary part of their growing acceptance of their new living space, the colonists, like Crichton, all wanted to be

6

on their way to their new destination.

'A few weeks circling the Earth won't make much difference,' Crichton had explained shortly after take-off. 'It is better that we become accustomed to our environment before we begin our main journey.'

The colonists, twenty men and twenty women, acknowledged the speech with only a small murmur of protest. Once you had accepted an undertaking like this, there was little point in becoming impatient. Being only the second ship to leave Earth, they had the best of everything: large quarters, their own social areas which included a bar and two different restaurants. They had exclusive access to their own swimming pool and gym. And, if any of them did feel inclined to breed before arriving at their destinations, there were facilities on board to deal with any babies and growing children. Of course the subsequent ships, soon to follow, would have fewer facilities and would be far more crowded. The smaller groups, containing the elite—or rather those that had paid for the privilege—were given the best of everything. Unlike the latter ships, that would contain fertile couples, who would mostly make up the workforce on the new world. Crichton knew all this as he spoke to them. He also knew that they should enjoy their time aboard *The Freedom* because things would be far tougher for all of them when they reached New Earth.

Crichton heard a piercing noise as the speakers buzzed in protest when he switched on the ship's com. *Thank God that's all we have to be concerned about,* he thought.

'Attention Colonists, First Officer Crichton speaking,' Crichton said when the screeching stopped. 'Apologies again for the small failure in the com system. The maintenance team are working to resolve this issue and I believe we can expect normal service to resume shortly. The first wave of colonists have been hugely successful in their terra-forming of New Earth. By the time we reach the planet there will be edible plant life, and proper homes for you to live in attached to the base. Soon you will see a new Sun burning brightly around a clean and unpolluted planet.'

Crichton didn't add that the pollution would come from the colonists themselves and, in many thousands of years, generations from now, New Earth would probably be ruined by humanity.

'This is a staff announcement. Can Chief Engineer Whitehawk please come to my office?' Crichton concluded.

Crichton switched off the com and another brief groan issued from the speakers. He grimaced then sat back in his chair. A few minutes later there was a knock on his office door.

Crichton checked his monitor to see Madison outside. He couldn't help

8

remembering the slender shape that she hid so well under the masculine overalls, or the brief kiss they had shared when he had followed her out of the Mess and down to her quarters. He let the memory of her pressed up against him, wearing nothing but the regulation grey vest and panties, float behind his eyes for a second. She looked steadily into the camera. Crichton was always amazed by how blue her eyes were against the faint tan skin and dark brown hair that reflected her Native American Indian heritage. There were so few people of her race left that it had been essential she was chosen for the trip.

Crichton saw their mission as something like Noah's Ark. The Earth was drowning in a sea of pollution, the atmosphere almost toxic: all due to the impending death of the sun. The plant-life that once provided the planet with oxygen, barely sustained a few enclosed cities. People lived inside pressure-sealed containers, with recycled air and oxygen pouring in. Experts had given the planet maybe thirty years to survive, but of course its occupants didn't know that. What the people had been told was that the Earth was overcrowded, that it needed time to recover, and that was why the colony was founded. This was completely untrue. The Earth was finished: there was nothing any of them could do, but the lie was there to quell the panic. They couldn't tell them that one day the sun would just snuff out

9

like an overused light bulb.

Years of searching had led them to the new planet in a solar system that was almost parallel to that of Earth. Of course the planet was different, with new plant life and possible bacteria that might be bad for humanity. But the chance had to be taken; otherwise they would *all* die when the final hours came.

Crichton pushed these morbid thoughts away as Madison entered. She looked confident and there was no sign that she was recalling their drinking session from the previous night.

'You wanted to see me?'

'You mean more of you than I saw last night?'

Madison smiled but it was humourless. 'Don't let the Captain know that you like slumming it over in *our* Mess.'

'There's no real action in the Officers' Mess. It's like a gentlemen's club with women. Unfortunately the ladies who frequent it are stuffier than the old guys.'

'You don't strike me as the type to have hung around that many gentlemen's clubs.'

Crichton smiled. 'I prefer less archaic company. So is there a game on tonight and are you playing?'

Madison folded her arms across her chest. Crichton now knew how much curve was under there but he said nothing.

'Nah. I think you cheat.'

Crichton's laugh burst from him in a natural and endearing ripple. Madison realised she liked it. It took a game of strip poker to get the measure of an officer sometimes. And to lighten him up.

'I like you Whitehawk,' he said. 'But back to business. There have been quite a few tech problems and I'd like to know what you're planning to do to resolve them.'

Madison almost sighed with relief. She had been worried that Crichton had brought her here for another reason. She wasn't that stoned that she didn't remember Crichton's moves the night before, nor that it was he who pulled away. She didn't want to think too much about how far she would have let things go because she knew the answer already. She liked Crichton. A lot. And part of her wondered if she had deliberately thrown the game to see where it led.

He was saving face for them both though by referring to the incident and then instantly talking shop. Madison wasn't sure exactly what this meant, but she considered it while she listened to Crichton speak; maybe he was embarrassed because he had been mixing with someone who was technically beneath his station. Or maybe he knew that this was the only way to dispel the awkwardness. Now that they had addressed it neither of them had to pretend it didn't happen.

'The system will be fixed by the end of the

day,' Madison said finally. 'Even if I do it myself.'

'Good,' Crichton said.

'One other thing . . . I've had complaints from the colonists that they can't communicate with their loved ones back home. What do I tell them?'

'Tell them that the system that was installed doesn't allow it,' Crichton said.

'But . . . the system does allow it . . . it's just blocked.' Madison said.

'I know. Look, it's best this way for all of them. Clean slate. That sort of thing.'

Madison said nothing as she took this information in. The fact was the system was blocked to everyone. She began to wonder why, but thought it best not to ask too many questions. It was still not too late to be ejected from the ship if she made waves.

'Very good, Sir. Is there anything else you wanted?'

Crichton's eyes swept over her and Madison noted how he shifted in his chair as though slightly uncomfortable. She blinked. Was she reading his expression correctly? She tried to focus on what he was saying about work, but she found herself watching him closely.

She had been wondering earlier if Crichton found her attractive. She knew the answer now.

Yes. He liked her. He really did.

Syra Connor stripped away her nightdress and pressed the start button on the exterior of the shower cubicle. A red scan-line ran the length of her body, top to bottom, assessing her temperature and the water began to flow. Syra stepped inside. As always the water was perfect.

'Body wash,' she said and the side jets issued a fine layer of soap that covered her skin. She began to lather the soap, enjoying the luxury as she recalled how her life had changed so much for the better.

Syra was not one of the privileged people who had automatically earned a chance at becoming some of the first colonists. She had lived in one of the worst ghettos: a dark, dank corner of London. She had heard about the colonisation programme on the grapevine and had gone to great lengths to send her DNA sample to the project. Even so, it was the equivalent of winning a lottery. The chances of being a perfect pair-match with one of the males, of being fertile, of holding the intelligence gene that all colonists needed . . . these things were so improbable that she had forgotten all about it as soon as she had submitted the tests.

Then the car had arrived for her: followed by a convoy of Security.

'Do you realise how special you are?' said a

voice from inside the car. 'You are a one in a million. If you agree to go to New Earth, then get inside the car. Leave your old life behind.'

That was when she saw Doctor Hallow for the first time.

She had looked back at the old and crumbling ruin of her home. The three-bedroom terraced house that she shared with her mother—it was barely airtight—and thought briefly whether she would miss anything inside.

'You must leave your old life. We will teach you to fit in,' said Hallow.

'What do I have to do?' she asked.

'It will mean a form of contract, between you and your pair-match. You will be expected to mate with him. Reproduce and care for children to help the future of the colony.'

Syra shrugged. Sex with someone she didn't know or care about didn't frighten her. It was a means to an end, sometimes a way of paying for food and living costs in the ghetto. She climbed inside the car and then Hallow introduced himself. He seemed friendly enough, and Syra accepted the drink and food he offered as they began their journey to the Centre.

'You are a very lucky young lady,' Hallow had said, placing his hand on her knee. 'We are going to take very good care of you. You and the other chosen will be the future of mankind.'

Syra had expected Hallow to make his move as the limousine joined the slow-moving motorway out of London. He did not, however, make a pass at her, removing his hand almost as quickly as he had placed it. That was when she realised just how important she was.

After that it had taken a year of preparation for the flight. Fitness assessments, a cocktail of vitamins to restore her nutrition levels to what they deemed healthy. Then of course there was a rigorous exercise regime.

'Shampoo,' Syra said, and then she stood still while the water jets above her stopped and the side body ones began. A measure of shampoo fell onto her hair and she began to massage and scrub until her pale blonde hair foamed up.

She thought about Ben Walsh. He was her companion and Syra wasn't that sure why or how the pairing was made, except that Hallow said it was something to do with their heritage. If she had been given the choice, Ben wouldn't have been it, though he was attractive enough. He was somewhat staid and Syra always felt as though she had to be on her best behaviour around him. It was difficult to relax in his company and he treated her as though he owned her. Even though the contract clearly stated that they were equal in all things. Sex with him was difficult. Ben wasn't very experienced. He was clumsy and Syra rarely

15

felt any satisfaction at all from their coupling.

'Rinse.'

Syra tilted her head as one of the shower jets above began to spray down onto her hair.

She loved the shower, the modern conveniences on board were better than anything she had experienced on Earth. Even once she joined the programme. When she asked for conditioner, however, something went wrong. Instead of the soft gel she expected, she had bubble bath deposited over her head and shoulders. The rinse mode stopped working and without any water to remove it, the soap stung her eyes. She staggered to the end of the cubicle, searching blindly for a towel, but the dispenser hadn't delivered it because the wash cycle was incomplete.

'Bloody Hell!'

Syra stumbled out of the shower and onto the carpet, then tripped over her slippers, landing face first on the floor. Her head struck the open doorway, a painful blow but not hard enough to daze her.

At that moment the safety alarm went off and Syra knew that a medical team would be hurrying towards her room. It was one of the benefits, and difficulties, of being a colonist: their wellbeing was constantly monitored.

She sat up, reached for her towelling robe and rubbed the soap from her eyes. Through watery, stinging slits she surveyed the chaos

16

of the room, the shower was intermittently coughing out water and soap and she was lying naked on the floor. She pulled the soiled robe on as two paramedics burst through into her living quarters.

'In here,' she called.

*   *   *

'I know you're responsible,' said Madison. 'I also understand why you did it.'

Priddy shrugged but didn't deny his involvement. They were in Madison's small office on the engine deck. As soon as he came in, Madison made him sit in the chair by the door. That way she could stand over him and look as though she was in charge. It was a technique she had been taught on the rigorous training for command she had endured for almost a year before the trip. She was the boss when it came to the mechanics of the ship and the men had to take her seriously.

'Have you fixed the com?' she asked.

'Yes. Loose bolt.'

'Right. So fix the shower unit and stop pranking around. It isn't funny. The comfort and safety of the colonists is *very* important.'

Priddy shrugged again. 'Just passing the time. Besides they are all so up themselves.'

'Pass the time in the social way, down in the Crew's Mess, not sabotage.'

'It's not sabotage, chief; it's just a little fun.

No real harm done.'

Madison sighed. If it wasn't for the fact that Priddy was a really good engineer, he would be travelling back to Earth right now in a cramped detention pod; all chances of ever getting to the new world completely blown.

'You're such a dick sometimes, Priddy. Your personal opinion of the colonists is tantamount to treason. Just count yourself lucky that the Captain doesn't know. I've told him we think it's space gremlins. But Priddy, you can't keep doing this. So get your ass over to the colonist sector and fix that shower. If I have one more complaint I'm going to have to cut you loose and tell the Captain what I know.'

'You'd *squeal* on me?'

'The girl slipped and banged her head. It could have been fatal. Don't you realise how serious this is?'

Priddy looked down, sighed and folded his arms. 'Sorry,' he said, but Madison wasn't sure she believed his apology. She was truly concerned that Priddy had a deep hatred for the colonists and she sighed internally, realising that she would need to supervise him closely in future.

'Come on. I'm going with you to fix that shower. It won't hurt for her to see someone is taking this seriously.'

A few minutes later they were standing outside Syra's rooms. When the door

18

opened, Priddy looked at Syra, now dressed, hair groomed, and a big red bruise on her forehead. Madison noticed how the young engineer blushed and looked down as the colonist invited them inside.

'Through here,' she said.

'It was a computer fault,' Madison explained. 'But Priddy will clean up the mess and check out that the system hasn't been damaged. I'm very sorry this happened to you, Miss Connor.'

'Its fine,' said Syra. 'Accidents happen. No real harm done.'

Priddy hurried into the bathroom and Madison glanced around the living space which was twice the size of those that had been allocated to the crew members. It reminded her of a luxury hotel suite. And indeed, Syra had everything here she could possibly need. A large lounge-diner, separate shower and bathroom leading into a large bedroom.

'All done,' said Priddy as he began to pack up his tools.

'Syra?' A male voice said from the bedroom.

Madison knew that the bedroom would also have another door which opened up into the bedroom of Syra's paired mate. She pushed the thought of it away. It was horrible really— like prostitution when you thought about it, even though it was deemed to be an honour.

Syra met Madison's eyes and frowned. Madison looked away. She knew she had given away her feelings about the colonists, but she couldn't take back the expression of pity that had been in her gaze.

'Syra?' said the male voice. Louder this time.

'If you've finished I have to go,' said Syra.

Priddy came out of the bathroom and Syra smiled at him. It wasn't flirty, but it was warm and it took the engineer by surprise.

'I'm so sorry,' said Priddy. 'But it's fixed now. It won't happen again.'

Madison found his reaction to Syra very interesting. His apology was sincere.

'Thank you.'

'What's going on in here?'

Syra flinched as Ben Walsh came into the lounge from the bedroom.

'There was a problem with the shower. It's fixed now.'

'My God what happened to your head?'

'I slipped. I'm fine. It's just a small bruise.'

Ben's face was filled with fury and arrogance. He was the kind of colonist that the engineers dreaded contact with.

'What carelessness. If she has been damaged . . .'

Syra put a hand on his arm and smiled. 'Ben . . . darling . . . I'm fine. The medics were here and they checked me over. It was just an accident.'

*   *   *

'I hope you're pleased with yourself,' Madison muttered as they waited for the lift to take them back down to engineering.

'She was really beautiful,' Priddy said. 'But what a jerk he was . . .'

Madison nodded. 'Hey. You aren't getting the hots for her are you? That is definitely way off-limits.'

Priddy laughed. 'Don't be stupid.'

2

Research

One Year Later

Joe Banks had harvested samples of all kinds of meteoroid, asteroid and other space debris that was routinely collected in the Catchers attached to the ship. His job was to take samples, analyse and report back anything that could be potentially hazardous to the occupants of the ship. Banks knew though that most of the rock he found, regardless of any bacteria, was completely harmless, but he suspected that the analysis team were looking for things that might be a latent risk for the settlers.

He checked the attachment on his lifeline.

'Banks? You ready?' asked Sasha Townsend through his head-com.

'Yep. Good job I'm an adrenaline junky . . .'

Sasha laughed. It was deep and throaty; Banks always enjoyed himself more if she was on the com during these expeditions into the ether. It made them less boring and routine.

'I'm opening the airlock. You sure you're attached?'

Banks tugged the line once more, checked the catch was in 'lock' and gave a thumbs up to the monitor beside him.

'Maybe one of these days you'll come and help tie me down.'

'You'd run a mile if I did,' Sasha laughed.

'Yeah. I reckon I would.'

The airlock slid open and Banks stepped forward. The inner door closed, and the air hissed out of the lock. Once the monitor light on the wall switched from red to green, Banks opened the outer door. It was a short leap down into the salvage tray from the airlock, but Banks paused to look out at the stars. He never failed to acknowledge the beauty of open space; it was something of a ritual for him. He tottered on the edge of the open airlock, looking down at the platform below. After a moment, arms outstretched he fell forward and down. He felt that wonderful weightlessness as he fell free but the feeling was short-lived, as he landed onto the platform within seconds.

His gloved fingers clasped the rail, and he pulled himself down, activating the magnets on the bottom of his boots.

The salvage tray was full of rocks that had been broken up as they were collected. Only small samples of the debris were brought in, and after analysis, the storage containers were purged, the rubble sent out into space once more. Banks bent down, looked over the edge into the pit, then flipped open a panel on the floor of the platform. He pulled a new, shorter, lifeline free, attached it to his belt, then unclipped the main line, snapping it onto the rail. Once secure, Banks reached for the top of the ladder and began his descent into the salvage pit. By the time he reached the bottom he was breathing heavily with the exertion of trying to walk normally in an anti-gravity environment. His visor steamed up briefly before the de-mist kicked in.

'You okay?' asked Sasha.

'Uh-huh.'

Banks stepped off the ladder and onto the debris. He walked around the clutter for a few moments, bending and examining various bits of rock.

'Nothing much of interest here,' he murmured.

Even so, his hand felt for a small hammer and pick that dangled from his belt on flexi-cord. In an anti-gravity situation it was hard to use these tools, but he was practised in letting the hammer's weight do the work for him. He bent towards the nearest rock and chipped off a small piece. He placed the shard in a pouch which was also attached to the belt. Then he stood up and made his way across the debris to the other side of the pit. Here he found more rock and something that appeared to be a flat piece of metal. He recognised the metal as the remnants of an old probe and pushed it aside. They were increasingly finding more and more garbage that had originated from space stations, satellites and probes. These were of no interest to him.

He was about to turn back when something caught his eye. It was flat and shiny. Banks bent down again, pushed aside bits of space crud with fat-gloved fingers. He tried to grasp it but the object eluded his clumsy hands. He kneeled down on the debris. It took him a moment to realise that the thing he was looking at was attached to the corner of a lump of meteoroid. It glittered like iron pyrite, better known as fool's gold.

'Strange,' he said.

'What is it?' asked Sasha through his com.

'Not sure.'

He used the hammer and pick and tapped the edge of the rock until a sliver of the glittering ore came free in a sharp triangle.

Banks stepped over to the ladder and began to climb back up to the platform. At the top of the platform, Banks unclipped the lifeline and fastened it back to his belt, then he re-stowed the short cord.

'Don't purge this pit until we've checked these samples,' he said.

'Putting a note on the system now,' Sasha answered.

'Reel me in,' he said.

This is a bit fast, he thought briefly as the open airlock door approached.

'Sasha. I'm coming in too quickly.'

'I know. There's something wrong. The computer should be controlling the speed and I can't make it stop!' The giggle had left her voice now. She was no longer enjoying herself and neither was Banks. It wasn't often that things went wrong, but when they did a few bruises were the least of the damage that he could hope for.

Banks missed the airlock and smashed into the side of the ship. His hands grabbed onto the hull grille. The impact winded him and it took a moment for him to regain enough breath to speak.

'I'm engaging the magnets,' Banks said when he could talk.

Banks made slow progress back to the airlock but when he finally crawled through the opening and the outer door closed behind him he felt himself relax. He was short of breath. The air in his suit felt thinner than usual.

An alarm sounded.

25

'What is it?' Banks asked gasping for air.

'You're losing pressure. I think your suit was damaged. I'm trying to balance the airlock and then you can take off your helmet, don't do it until . . . Banks? Banks? What are you doing? We haven't quarantined the samples . . .'

Sasha forgot all about the rules in her panic. She was afraid that Banks was going to die if she didn't help him. She ran from the control room, down the corridor and threw herself on the emergency unlock. The half-pressurised room sucked air in from the corridor. Sasha staggered for a moment, then as the pressure balanced she hurried towards Banks. He was clawing at his helmet, eyes bulging as he slowly suffocated. With trembling fingers Sasha unfastened the locks and pulled the helmet off.

Banks felt the air hit his face. Sweat dried on his cheeks and forehead as he gulped in big breaths. He felt as though a thousand ants were crawling inside his suit. He wriggled and squirmed.

'Get me out of this . . .' he gasped.

'What's wrong?' Sasha asked.

His hand throbbed. Banks dropped the rock shard. It glittered on the floor beside him. Sasha stared at it. Her eyes fell on his glove. A thin trickle of blood dripped from a one-inch long gash in the material.

Banks felt nauseous. His arm ached and he felt as though something was crawling inside his hand. It moved up past his wrist and slowly pulled itself through the inside of his arm. He swatted at it. Screamed. Then pushing Sasha aside, he rolled over, smashing his body around the airlock as though he were fighting an invisible demon.

Sasha backed out of the airlock, pressed the emergency lock and sent an alarm up to the Bridge.

'Sasha what is it?' asked Captain Fence.

'Banks . . .' was all she could say because she didn't know how to describe what had happened.

Inside the airlock, Banks sank down onto the floor in one corner. His eyes blank. Legs splayed out. He looked like a rag-doll abandoned by a spoilt child.

*　　　*　　　*

'How is he?' asked Captain Fence.

'In a coma.'

Doctor Hallow and Fence stood beside a glass window that looked into the medical quarantine area. Fence was in his full uniform of grey and black. His hair was shorn in the military preferred crew cut. Still in his early thirties, he kept himself in peak condition: as did all the crew. There wasn't a man among them over the age of thirty five and all of the women were under thirty.

'Has anyone analysed the shard?' Fence

27

asked.

'It's undergoing tests at the moment. So far nothing unusual has come up. Banks is suffering from oxygen deprivation; hopefully he'll recover. We are still gathering information.'

'Keep me informed.'

Hallow stared long and hard into the room even as Fence walked away. Banks knew better than to make such a stupid mistake. He should have put the shard away in the belt sack. That would have freed his hands and this wouldn't have happened.

'Is he going to be okay, Doc?' asked Sasha as she joined him at the window.

'His vitals are steady but he hasn't woken up. We don't know how long he will be like this, but sometimes a coma isn't a bad thing, Sasha. It gives the brain time to heal.'

Hallow paused. 'You broke protocol opening the airlock.'

'I had to get to him. He was suffocating. Besides . . . it was just a standard meteoroid. Nothing too risky. We're moving to a whole new planet and I'm sure we'll come across far worse . . .'

'That's not the point Sasha, and you know it. Did you go through decontamination?'

'Look, I'm fine Doc. It's Banks we need to be worried about. The Captain has read me the riot act already. I don't need any more lectures today.'

28

Hallow sighed. 'Okay. Just let me know immediately if you suffer any ill effects.'

'I will.'

Sasha walked away and turned left at the end of the corridor. She was heading over to the sanitization area to take the decontamination shower, but there was no point in telling Hallow that—he would only freak and insist her whole department was locked up like Banks was going to be, even if he did wake up with his brain intact.

In the decontamination chambers, Sasha set the showers to remote, then dropped her clothing into the incinerator, stepped into the shower and walked onto the conveyor. The floor began to move, pulling her through the chemical shower and light therapy bombardment. When she reached the other end she took a pair of blue pyjamas and pulled them on. Then she made her way back to her cabin.

By the time she reached her room she was feeling nauseous. It had been incredibly unsettling to see Banks almost suffocate. If she hadn't helped him remove the helmet she was sure he would have died outright. The thought of not helping him, of the alternative scenario, made her stomach turn even more.

She keyed in her pass-code, entered her room, then sank down on her sofa.

'Lights off,' she said. The room plunged into darkness and Sasha fell into a heavy sleep.

3

Love-sick

'What's got into you?' Madison asked as she entered the engine control room and found Priddy combing his hair.

Normally his fingernails held traces of engine grease, and there was a smell that followed him around because he didn't get his overalls cleaned regularly enough. But now his fingers were clean, his hair washed, he smelt of aftershave and he wasn't wearing his usual stained uniform.

'I'm off duty for a few days . . . but I got called in to check the colonists' shower systems again. Seems like we've had some computer failure in sector five.'

'Oh Priddy . . . what did you do?'

'Not me. I swear. Learnt my lesson last year. Thought I might be able to help though.'

'Let someone else do it if you're on leave,' Madison said.

'I don't mind. I'd rather check it out . . . just in case . . .'

'Just in case it really is *still* your fault. You really pissed me off over this last year, Priddy. I hope you realise that and don't make me regret letting it pass.'

Priddy opened his locker and took out his

tool box.

'I'll check it out then let my holiday start . . . okay? There seems to be a blockage in one of the showers. It might be related but probably isn't.'

Madison let him go. At least seeing the colonist injured had curbed his prankster ways. And he was trying to make sure that it hadn't had a knock on effect to the system which made her consider how concerned he really was.

Madison checked the settings for the bathroom systems for the colonists' floor. It all looked okay but the air-conditioning unit in sector three was showing an abnormality. She keyed in the diagnostic codes and watched as the computer found and solved the slight anomaly.

'Did you hear about Banks?' asked Gill as he and Tory Ansell entered the computer room.

Madison nodded. 'He's always been a bit of a maverick. I can't help wondering what foolish moves led him to disaster.'

'You're a hard woman. The man could be brain-damaged,' Gill said.

'I don't wish that on him, obviously. But accidents are mostly caused by carelessness and are avoidable. Naturally I want Banks to recover,' Madison said.

'He's in quarantine too,' Tory said. 'Poor Banks. He's a great guy, but I know what you mean about him being a rebel. When we were in training, I saw him throw himself out of a twenty foot sky-scraper with only a rubber rope attached to his ankles.'

'They call that bungee jumping. It was a twenty-first century extreme sport,' Gill explained. 'Banks said it gave him the same feeling as propelling yourself out into space. I think he was doing it for training as well as the thrill.'

'Whatever it was, it scared the hell out of me just watching him,' Tory said.

'Hey. What's that?' asked Gill.

'What?' asked Tory.

'A blip on the computer. The air-conditioning units.'

'I just checked those. There was a problem but the computer said it was resolved.'

Madison returned to the monitors. 'What is it doing? Damn! One of the air recycling units is defective. Gill, get your tools. You and I are going down into the system to take a look.'

*   *   *

Priddy stood outside of Syra's door for several minutes before he could gather the nerve to knock. He still felt guilty that his prank had caused her harm. Some of the colonists deserved a little put down but Syra was nice. She hadn't made a fuss at all—unlike her male partner Walsh. The truth was, Priddy hadn't found anything wrong with the showers but he had wanted an excuse to return. He had been thinking about Syra ever since he first met her a year ago. And, although he had caught glimpses of her when he was working around the ship, he hadn't been able to pluck up courage to actually talk to her again. After a while the urge had become something of an obsession that he could no longer ignore. It was crazy and it would do him no good but he *had* to talk to her again and this was the only time he could ever legitimately have contact with her.

He finally rapped on the door and when Syra opened it, and not her mate, he was relieved.

She was wearing the colonists' uniform. A pale blue jumpsuit that fitted her curves in all of the right places. Priddy's eyes swept over her but he disguised his interest by lowering his head in a bow.

'I'm sorry to disturb you, miss. But this is a follow-up on the problems you had. I just wanted to check the system was now working properly. Could I possibly come in and take a look?'

Syra stepped back, 'Of course.'

Priddy entered the suite and waited as Syra closed the door.

'How are you now, miss?'

'I'm very well, thank you,' Syra said and smiled. 'It's kind of you to ask.'

Priddy blushed, then nodded and walked towards the bathroom door. 'With your permission?'

Syra nodded.

Inside the bathroom, Priddy checked out the system, knowing that all would be well and then he returned to the lounge to find Syra sitting reading on the sofa. She held something that he had only ever seen in a museum. It was an actual book, not a digireader.

Syra placed the book down on the sofa and looked up at Priddy.

'How is everything?'

'All okay, miss,' Priddy said.

'Thank you for looking after my shower,' Syra said. 'What's your name?'

'Priddy.'

'Please call me Syra. I'm just the same as you.'

Priddy blinked.

'We are all humans. *All* colonists. I don't understand the need for this ridiculous divide,' Syra was saying. 'Why you feel you have to bow to me for example. I'm from the worst bloody ghetto in . . .'

'I think you are beautiful,' Priddy said.

Syra smiled. *You're my type too*, she thought but didn't dare voice her thoughts. *Not that stuffed-shirt they've paired me with.*

'I assume you have a first name?'

'Dave . . . but no one uses it.'

'Dave it is then.'

34

4

Banks Awakes

Banks opened his eyes and looked up at the plastic sheeting over his bed. He turned his head slowly, a wave of sickness followed the movement and he was forced to close his eyes. In those few seconds he had seen that the whole area surrounding his bed was walled off by sheets of clear plastic. He felt confused and dizzy. He couldn't remember where he was or how he came to be there. He tried to sit up but the dizziness got worse and he fell back onto the pillows, waiting for the room to stop spinning around him.

Banks felt strange. His mouth was dry, his throat was tight and he couldn't remember his own name. The thought terrified him. He tried to speak but no sound came out of his mouth.

Think! Where are you? Okay this looks like a hospital bed, so something must have happened.

He began to remember unimportant things, memories that had no particular meaning or significance. A glass of water stood on a table; a spider climbing up the wall of a crumbling old building; a small child crying, rubbing his eyes with tiny fists. The images floated behind his eyes in a jumbled mess but meant *nothing*.

He opened his eyes and looked around,

35

turning his head slowly from side to side. On one side of the bed was a heart monitor. He considered this knowledge and understood that the wires and tubes he saw were somehow attached to him. So his brain wasn't completely wiped of knowledge, just some things were there. Yes. Definitely a hospital. But where?

His mind stumbled around for any knowledge or memory that was personal. He recalled a face. A pretty girl looking down on him and there was a helmet being removed. Who was she?

Banks tried to remember her voice—he felt it was important, but he couldn't recall it at all. He saw her mouth move. She was speaking but the sound, the words, were gone.

He slid up against the pillows, slowly pulling himself up into a sitting position. The room began to spin again. He froze, closed his eyes and swallowed even though his mouth was still dry. After a few seconds the spinning stopped. There was a fugue around him, like a thick invisible fog of confusion, but at least the room was static again when he opened his eyes.

Banks felt nausea tug at his insides. A wave of sickness rolled up his stomach but he choked it back.

'Nurse!' he croaked. His hand reached out. On some subliminal level he knew where the call button was. He pressed and held until a figure lifted the plastic curtain and came in.

Banks stared up at the biohazard suited

figure. Judging by height and shape, Banks thought it was a man.

'Sick . . .' he said.

A bowl was placed before him. Banks let the vomit come and heaved into the basin until his insides hurt, and his throat was raw. The man in the suit held him up until the sickness subsided, then he lowered him back against the pillows.

'How do you feel?' asked a muffled voice.

Banks wasn't sure if the voice was muffled because of the suit the man was wearing or whether his hearing was wrong.

'Water . . .' he croaked.

'Slowly . . .' said the nurse.

Banks sipped at the water. It tasted like the bile that had spewed from his stomach and so he found himself heaving again.

'I'm sending for Doctor Hallow,' said the nurse.

His ears were clearing now, and so was the blurred fog around his eyes. He found himself staring into the clear plastic mask that the nurse was wearing. He didn't recognise the man, but thought he should know him. He searched around in his brain, accessing his memories like a hacker in a computer.

'Evans . . .' Banks said.

'Yes. That's me. The doctor's on his way. It will take him some time to suit up. You've been very sick. We weren't sure you'd wake up.'

37

'Sick? What happened?'

'You don't remember?'

The hacker routed around again. 'Meteoroid . . .' he lifted his hand before his face and looked down at the cut on his palm. It was a long red gash that appeared to be mostly healed.

'Yes. Don't worry buddy, it will all come back to you.'

The nurse didn't notice how Banks examined his hand as though he had never seen fingers before.

'You've been out for over a week so I'm not surprised you're confused.'

'What's my name?' Banks asked.

'Lay back and let me check your vitals. Then when the Doc gets here I'm sure you'll have the answers you need.'

Banks lay back and patiently let Evans monitor his blood pressure and check his temperature.

'You're burning a little too high so I'm going to up your dose of meds.'

'I'm fine,' said Banks. 'It's just a little warm in here.'

'Yeah. I know. At least this suit has aircon,' Evans laughed.

Banks closed his eyes and drifted once more into a strange half-sleep, where his thoughts and memories drifted behind his lids. Some of the pieces made sense, while others didn't.

'I'm Banks,' he murmured.

Evans covered the vomit bowl, then placed it in a sealed box to send down to the lab. Looking at Banks though, Evans thought the man was on the road to recovery. He would soon be out of quarantine and back to work. It was like Hallow said: oxygen deprivation. That would certainly explain the memory loss and confusion.

*　　　*　　　*

'Heard you were awake,' said Sasha.

Banks opened his eyes. He was in a normal ward now: a small room with four beds but he was the only person in there.

'Sasha,' he said.

Sasha smiled. She was pleased that he recognised her because she had been told of his memory issues.

'Hey. How are you feeling?'

'More alert. Happy to be out of quarantine.'

'I know. They went a bit overboard on that I think, keeping you in there for a week when you were unconscious anyway.' Sasha said.

Her hand was resting on his wrist. Banks turned his arm and let her hand fall into his palm. He squeezed a little. Sasha couldn't help noticing how warm his hand was. Hot in fact. She pulled away as soon as it seemed polite.

'I believe I have you to thank for saving me.'

Sasha's eyes clouded over and Banks knew then how close the call had been. 'It was nothing. You'd have done the same for me.'

'And how are you feeling?' Banks asked.

'Me? I'm fine. Why?'

'No loss of memory?'

Sasha laughed. 'I had decontamination sickness for a few days. I don't recommend that to anyone. God knows what's in that chemical shower. I think I'm more likely to get cancer from that lot than some strange bug from outer-space.'

Banks smiled slowly. 'Bug?'

'You know. Bacteria. But we are both okay anyway. Aren't we?'

'Yes,' said Banks. 'They are letting me out today. 'Do you know what caused the malfunction on the safety wire?'

'Computer glitch. We don't know why but these things just keep happening. If we were on Earth you could probably sue someone for negligence . . . but . . .'

Banks laughed, then became shy as he said, 'Should be able to go to my own cabin this afternoon. Can't wait to sleep in my own bed. Will you come round for a drink? As a thank you?'

'Sure. But should you be drinking?'

Banks smiled. 'One little drink won't hurt.'

*　　*　　*

Banks opened his eyes again. He was in his cabin, sitting on his sofa. A row of small bowls

40

containing snacks and a bottle of synth-Jack Daniels whiskey stood on a small coffee table with two glasses.

He looked around the room. Everything was as he remembered. The room was like all the crew rooms. A studio apartment layout meaning that living, sleeping and eating space was all combined in one room. In the corner was a bed, partitioned off with a thin plastic wall. Over in the other corner was a small kitchenette with fridge and cooker. Then there was the sitting area containing a two-seater sofa and a monitor from where he could stream entertainment. Banks recalled that every movie and television show ever made up to the point of them leaving Earth was archived on this system but it felt as though he were seeing these things for the first time.

To the left of the front door was a small bathroom. The crew didn't have the luxury of baths; unlike the colonists. All they had were showers.

Banks couldn't remember being discharged from the infirmary, or arriving back in his room. Nor could he recall preparing the snacks for Sasha's arrival; yet there they were. The last thing he remembered was inviting her over.

He shrugged. It didn't matter. Hallow had said he was on the mend, though for now work was off and he just had to let the recovery happen. They had tested him. Found nothing physiologically wrong. The memory loss would improve. It already had. Over the last couple of days since he woke he felt he had re-experienced his entire life. There were still the blank moments though.

'It's nothing to be concerned with,' Hallow had said. 'I think it's when your brain gets overloaded with the returning memories. You go on auto-pilot. Blank out, but still function. Or perhaps what is really happening is that you are forgetting your new memories. Either way I'm hoping that you will fully recover given time.'

'What if I don't?' Banks had asked.

'We'll cross that bridge when we come to it,' Hallow said. 'Just rest up. Try establishing a normal routine, and then we'll talk about you returning to light duties. No more throwing yourself from the ship for a while though. Okay?'

Banks had felt a little reassured but couldn't shake the feeling that he was somehow not inside himself during these moments. It felt disjointed. And though he had learnt to access his thoughts and remember other things there were periods that remained a complete blank.

The chime rang on his door bell. He remembered that it was the same as the one on his apartment back on Earth.

'Hi,' said Sasha as Banks opened the door.

Banks stepped back and Sasha entered his cabin.

'This place is great,' she said. 'It looks *just* like mine.'

They both laughed and Banks poured a generous measure of the whiskey into the two glasses.

'Ice?' he asked.

'Sure,' Sasha said.

Banks walked over to the fridge.

She wandered around his room taking in his personal possessions. On the computer desk she saw the picture of a woman and a little boy.

'Family?' she asked.

Banks glanced up from the ice cube dispenser. He stared across the room and frowned as though he had trouble accessing the memory.

'My sister and her boy . . .'

'She's pretty.'

Banks pushed one of the glasses under the dispenser. Two large lumps of ice dropped down into the whiskey.

'I think they have a place on the next ship. Actually, that will most likely be on its way now.'

'Yes,' Sasha said. 'I heard the launch was a success. Good news that they are only six months behind us. So you'll have chance to settle in on New Earth before they arrive.'

Banks held out the glass of Jack and ice and Sasha took it. She filled the momentary awkward silence by sipping the drink.

'Nice. Haven't had this stuff for ages.'

'It was my little indulgence. I have several bottles in storage. They will only come out for special occasions like this.'

'Yep. You getting better is definitely a special occasion.'

Sasha raised her glass and Banks chinked his against hers.

'I'll drink to that. Plus . . .' Banks paused. 'It's nice to have you over.'

Sasha sat down on the sofa and reached for the nearest bowl. It contained black olives. She took one and began to chew.

'Nice to be here. You expecting any of the other guys? Only there are enough snacks here . . .'

Banks smiled. 'I don't entertain much and I wasn't sure what you'd like.'

He sat down on the sofa beside her, 'I'm very grateful to you.'

Then he leaned closer and placed a kiss on Sasha's cheek.

Sasha had always liked Banks—much more than any of the other available men on board. It wouldn't hurt to see where this led. After all, the world would end if they didn't all reproduce, wouldn't it? Deep down she had been hoping he liked her, but had been too afraid at the beginning of the journey to show any interest in anyone. She had, first and foremost, wanted to be recognised for her work quality. Now though she didn't see any harm in exploring her feelings for Banks.

Sasha turned her head and let Banks kiss her. It was nice, even though his skin was still very hot. His tongue rubbed against her lips and she opened her mouth, then pulled him closer as a warm surge of lust rippled through her. She had almost forgotten what sex was like. He wrapped his arms around her waist and pulled her close. The kiss grew deeper and Sasha relaxed into it enjoying the warmth of his tongue as it explored her mouth.

Then there was another feeling. Something strange and alien in her mouth. A slimy lump wriggled from him and into her mouth. Sasha tried to pull away but Banks' arms were like a vice around her waist and his tongue continued to work inside her mouth until she was forced to swallow whatever the thing was. He suddenly released her and she fell back against the sofa, coughing and heaving.

She had a flash of memory. Some years ago her brother had dared her to place a maggot in her mouth when they had gone fishing. Sasha had done it. But after spitting out the wriggling disgusting thing she had felt sick and dirty. Whatever she had just swallowed felt just like that maggot and she imagined it squirming down inside her.

'What the hell was that Banks?' she gasped. 'Is this some kind of joke?'

'Banks isn't here right now but I have his memories,' said Banks.

He pushed her back onto the sofa. Then stretched out over her. Sasha was feeling sick again. A strange sensation was swirling around in the pit of her stomach as though something writhed there.

'I feel sick,' she said.

'It will pass.'

'You're frightening me.'

'You came here to procreate.'

Sasha tried to laugh. It was pretty funny when put so formally, but yes—she had known, and perhaps hoped, that the evening would lead to this.

'Stop jerking me around then,' she said. 'What did you push in my mouth?'

'Nothing,' said Banks.

The queasiness was gone now and she began to feel stronger. Her body temperature was changing too. Banks no longer felt too hot to her touch. The heat was sensual and a burning need began to pound in her chest, throbbed in her temples and sent fire through her body.

'See. You're fine,' murmured Banks against her mouth even though she was now reluctant to kiss him.

Banks ran his hands over her arms. His touch sent tingling sensations all over her skin. She let him unzip her top and pull away the uniform trousers.

*   *   *

46

In the morning Sasha dressed and Banks watched her leave. He said nothing, he was afraid to. He couldn't remember what had happened between them and he was scared he may offend her. Even so, he felt more like himself than he had since he first woke in quarantine.

'Procreate . . .' Sasha said from the doorway. Her voice sounded strange. 'Go forth and multiply.'

Banks had no idea what she was talking about. As she closed the door behind her, he turned over in the bed and fell immediately back to sleep. He dreamt of small translucent worms. They wriggled up his arms, and burrowed into his skin reproducing inside him until he was nothing more than an incubator.

An hour later Banks woke up screaming. He staggered from his bed and into the bathroom. He stared at his jaundiced skin. Blood leaked from his nose. He pulled a wad of toilet tissue from the roll and pressed it to his nose but it continued to fill with blood. He blew it once, a torrent of clotted blood filled the paper. He dropped the tissue into the toilet bowl. As the toilet began its automatic flush, Banks glanced down. He thought he saw something white wriggling to the surface and then it was gone.

He stumbled back into his room, collapsed on his chair and picked up the remote control for his monitor.

'Gotta rest. Maybe should have stayed off

the whiskey last night . . .'

His eyes fell on the bottle of Jack and the two still full glasses on the coffee table. Then a flash of memory came back into his head. He remembered the kiss and then . . .

Banks put his head in his hands. The scar across his palm throbbed against his cheek.

'What the hell is happening to me?' he said.

5

Technical Problems

'It looks like sabotage,' Madison confided to Gill. 'I hope Priddy isn't responsible for this.'

'Come on. Why would Priddy . . .? Why would anyone on-board do this? They'd die too and let's be honest, suffocation isn't a nice way to go.'

'I know you're right Gill. But how else can you explain it? The fan shouldn't be broken. It looks like something smashed it up,' Madison said.

'Something? What a strange thing to say.'

Madison sighed. 'I'm feeling pretty freaked by this. It's been a long journey already and we have several years to pass before we get to New Earth. I just don't want any more of these things to conk out on us. We only have so many parts we can use.'

'Chill. We're okay. It's fixed and this is just space scrap,' said Gill placing his arm around her shoulders. It wasn't often he saw any cracks in Madison's composure and he felt sympathy for her because he knew she took the flack from above.

'What's this?'

Madison looked up to see Crichton standing in the doorway of the repairs room.

'Aircon failure. We've fixed it now,' said Gill dropping his arm away.

'The Captain wants a full report on this Engineer Whitehawk,' Crichton said. 'Excuse us, Gill.'

Gill glanced at Madison then left the room. Crichton closed the door behind him.

'I'll get the report done as quickly as possible. I'm still trying to come up with a reasonable explanation. So far I'm failing.'

'We seem to be jinxed,' Crichton shrugged.

'Is Captain Fence really mad about this?' Madison asked.

'No. I doubt he'll even read your report. All he cares about is keeping the ship running. If that's happening, then there's no real problem.'

'But you've come down here to rag my ass anyway?'

Crichton smiled, 'That's such an intriguing idea.'

'Get out of here . . .' she laughed.

'Later?' Crichton said.

49

Madison smiled.

'Is that a yes?' Crichton asked.

Whenever they found themselves alone, Madison became awkward, but never rejected Crichton's flirtation. She enjoyed it, but wasn't sure what it meant.

'What did you have in mind?' she said.

'A little drink?'

Madison looked down at the broken fan again. Was it worth worrying about if Fence and Crichton weren't too concerned?

'I'm not sure,' she said.

'It's only a drink . . .' Crichton said.

Madison looked up, 'I meant . . . Never mind.'

'What are you afraid of?' Crichton asked.

'If the world wasn't dying I guess I'd be saying it would be unprofessional of us to start something.'

'Those rules hardly apply now. We're off to a new world. We make our own rules. The only person we answer to is the Captain and he is already marking his territory with one of the Bridge crew. It's only a matter of time before he acts on it.'

Madison was a little taken aback by this information. She had heard that Fence was married. Though it was strange his wife hadn't come on the trip with them. Even so she thought Crichton's comment was cynical. He had an attitude to pairing that Madison couldn't quite share. Maybe in time she would feel the same but for now she didn't want to make any mistakes.

She liked Crichton, but she didn't trust his motives. The rules of dating had changed some time ago and fertile females could now take their pick of the men. She didn't want to commit to a pairing so soon. If she became pregnant to Crichton then the decision would be taken from her.

'I'm not ready for any commitment,' she said.

'Neither am I. But I'm very interested in knowing more about you,' Crichton said.

'Just a drink then?'

'I promise,' said Crichton.

*   *   *

Sasha looked at the digireader in her hand. It was all squiggles and lines. The words meant nothing to her. Sometimes she covered for Engineer Dirk on the Bridge and at those times it was her job to make sure that the ship's communications were monitored for anything coming from the colony or Earth. Today, however, his report looked like a foreign language.

'What are you trying to pull?' she asked.

'What?' said Dirk.

'I can't read this.'

Dirk glanced down at the tablet, 'My handwriting isn't that bad. But if you are having trouble just change it to typed mode.'

Sasha forced her mind to focus. The shapes stopped moving on the page, but she felt something shift inside her head instead. She experienced a momentary discomfort, a sharp pain that was gone as quickly as it came, then the words formed. She pressed her hand against her temple.

'Yeah . . . you should have been a doctor,' she joked. 'It's okay. I can *just* make it out.'

Dirk grinned and walked away.

Sasha placed the tablet down on the desk and picked up the com-link, carefully placing it in her ear. She sat down and switched on the links. There was some white noise, then the communications channels cleared. She spoke the protocols down each of the lines to check the connections were open and working then waited for the automated responses.

On the monitor screen beside her she could see the open blackness outside. The area around them was clear. No sign of meteoroid or space debris. Sasha felt pain again and sickness when she recalled Banks and the accident. Her mind stumbled over the previous evening. She wondered if Banks had put something in her drink. Since she woke up and found herself in his bed she had been tripping over half-remembered fragments. She recalled flashes of a terrible nightmare and maggot things crawling through her body.

'Sasha?'

52

'Captain Fence?'

The Captain was standing by the desk and she hadn't even seen him approach.

'The report please.'

Sasha looked down at the tablet, it was now full of her own handwriting. She glanced at the clock. Four hours had passed and it felt as though she had only just arrived to take up her post. She passed the tablet to Fence.

'You've been very quiet today,' Fence said.

Sasha didn't know what to respond but she smiled at the Captain instead. He was always nice to her and they had established a form of banter when they were alone on the Bridge.

'Had a lot on my mind,' Sasha said.

'I hope you're not still worrying about your friend, Banks. Hallow says he's well on the road to recovery.'

'I was, Captain. Thanks for asking. Banks is getting better now.'

'Good.'

Sasha liked the Captain. She wanted to touch him suddenly. She wondered if his body was warm or cool. She reached out her hand to stroke his hair.

The Bridge door opened. Sasha pulled back her hand as Dirk came in, followed by Crichton. Sasha was soon involved in the handover with Dirk and she noticed too that the Captain was being relieved by Crichton.

'Time for sleep,' Fence said as they both exited the Bridge.

'I feel tired,' Sasha said. 'But I also have this insane urge for something strong to drink.'

They entered the lift. Sasha pressed the button for her floor and waited for the Captain to press his level.

'Do you have anything strong in your quarters?' Fence asked.

'I have a little something for special occasions,' she said.

Fence said nothing for a moment, 'So. Your friendship with Banks . . .?'

'Purely platonic,' Sasha said. Part of her mind objected to the lie but she couldn't stop herself from saying it.

The doors opened on the crew deck. Sasha glanced at Fence. The Captain seemed uncertain for a moment and then he followed her down the corridor to her cabin. He glanced around nervously until she opened her door. Inside she called for the lights and the room was illuminated.

Fence knew what the crew cabins looked like. His was slightly bigger but not by much.

'How are you feeling?' Sasha asked.

'Guilty.'

Sasha said nothing. Instead she pulled an unopened bottle of wine from under her sink. She placed two glasses down on the kitchen work surface.

'I left my wife behind. She didn't pass the fertility tests.'

'I know,' said Sasha. 'We all left someone

54

who wasn't suitable. But they may make it over on the final civilian ships.'

'There will only ever be the colonists' ships.'

'What do you mean?'

Fence rubbed his head. 'It doesn't matter if you know, or if everyone else on board finds out knows the truth.'

'What truth?'

'The powers that be have known for a long time that Earth is doomed.'

'We know the planet is dying. But that will be a hundred years from now . . .'

'No. Twenty to thirty tops.'

'Oh my God. That's why we don't have direct contact with Earth isn't it?'

Fence nodded, 'Yes. They are afraid that we'll tell family members.'

'Is that why you feel guilty? Because everyone still there will probably die if they don't make it onto one of the ships?'

'No one infertile will get on any of the ships, regardless of who they are.'

Sasha placed her glass down on the work top and she walked towards the Captain. 'I have family back home that fall into that category. But you know what, we shouldn't feel guilty for surviving. Survival is important to us now.'

They looked at each other and the moment was so awkward that Fence put his glass down too. 'I shouldn't have come here. Sorry.'

'Captain,' Sasha said catching hold of his

arm. 'What can I do to ease the guilt?'

6

Hunger

Banks was hungry. The pain gnawed at his stomach. He struggled up from the sofa and staggered over to the kitchen area. He opened his cupboards, then remembered that he hadn't been to the stores to stock up because of his accident. He looked at his arms. They seemed thinner than before and he couldn't remember the last time he had eaten anything.

He headed for the door, and then realised that he was still in his sleepwear. For a moment he was confused and didn't know what to do. He realised that it would be inappropriate to go outside like this. His brain suddenly registered that he had to shower and dress.

He caught sight of himself in the bathroom mirror as he reached for his toothbrush. His mouth was thick and furry. His hair was sticking to his head; eyes were bloodshot. His lips were white and bloodless and his skin looked jaundiced in the yellow light of the room. *Jesus, I look awful. Maybe I ought to go and see the Doc . . .*

He shook his head. The thought of being

back in the hospital didn't appeal to him on any level. He had an innate fear of being put back into quarantine. Instead he pushed the toothbrush into his mouth, cleaned his teeth and ran the brush over his tongue in the hope that the bilious taste would disappear. The minty paste made him feel sick though, and as he rinsed his mouth with water that tasted like poisonous metal, Banks began to realise that maybe something was seriously wrong with him after all. *I should get help.*

He switched on the shower. As he peeled away his clothing a rank scent wafted from his yellowed skin and made him gag. The water felt cold, but he forced himself to endure the discomfort as he tried to wash away the awful stink. He smelt like rotting flesh. There was no other way to describe it and the smell, as well as the hunger, frightened him more than anything had in his life.

His body was so sensitive that the towel felt like sandpaper as he rubbed himself dry. When Banks pulled on his uniform the fabric seemed to chaff his skin but he forced himself to dress anyway.

He looked at himself in the mirror, then combed his now clean hair. He looked and smelt better but his watery eyes were still wrong and there was nothing he could do about it.

The hunger gripped his stomach again. He lurched forward heaving over the sink. Pain

57

shot up into his head as a trickle of blood dripped out of his nose again. He wiped it away with the back of his hand. Once again the thought of calling for help crossed his mind, but no sooner had he thought it than a twitch occurred in his brain and the urge was dampened.

Outside in the corridor he forced himself to walk confidently towards the Mess. He passed two of his colleagues, but kept his eyes on the floor and didn't acknowledge them. He was surprisingly grateful that they did not try to engage him in conversation.

With every step closer to the Mess Banks became more certain that he would feel better if he ate something. He had been careless and stupid since coming out of the infirmary. He hadn't taken care of himself at all. Forgetting to eat and drink was bound to cause him difficulty in space.

He entered the Mess, picked up a tray and went straight to the buffet. The food offering didn't look too appetising.

'Hey, Banks!' said Gill. 'How are you feeling?'

'Hungry,' said Banks.

'Good sign. Come over and join us if you want.'

Banks nodded. He glanced over his shoulder to see Tory, Gill, Priddy and Madison sitting at the corner table. He didn't want to join them but knew it would be odd if he went to another table.

He looked down at the food. Beef. Yes. He wanted meat. His mouth watered as he reached for the bowl. Then he picked up all of the accompaniments and a bottle of water before turning and walking over to the table.

His eyes fell on Tory as he sat down. The hunger roared in his stomach again and his guts cramped up. He also felt strangely attracted to the girl, which was odd because he had always thought her dull and uninteresting. Unlike Sasha.

'You okay?' asked Tory.

Banks didn't answer. He focused his eyes on the food and began to eat it with his fingers.

'Let me get you a fork,' Gill said, standing up. Banks didn't notice the look he exchanged with Madison and Priddy, or the fact that Tory was staring at him.

Gill placed a fork on the table but Banks ignored it and continued to shovel in the food without looking up.

The four engineers tried to continue their conversation.

'So. The fan is replaced, but we don't need any more disasters on this journey,' Madison said.

'Y . . . Yeah . . .' said Tory, distracted by Banks' eating habits. 'There's enough freaky shit to deal with around here right now.'

Banks picked up a dessert bowl containing what looked like a strawberry sponge pudding with custard. He looked around, then he saw the fork beside him and picked it up. He stabbed the fork into the bowl, but seemed unable to scoop any of the dessert out.

The engineers fell silent and watched him. Banks looked up. The whites of his eyes were as yellow as his skin and more blood leaked from his nostrils, making a trail to his top lip.

Tory couldn't help herself. She jumped out of her chair and backed away.

'Shit, Banks. You really don't look too good. You're bleeding . . .'

Gill and Priddy stood slowly and went around the table.

'Let's get you back to the infirmary,' said Priddy. 'Get Doc Hallow to take a look at you.'

'Just hungry,' muttered Banks.

'Seriously, dude,' said Gill. 'You look like shit.'

'You're such a charmer, Gill,' said Madison.

Banks put his head down into the bowl and began to slurp the custard and cake into his mouth. Tory moved around the table and stood behind Madison, who remained seated.

'Call the Doc,' said Madison.

Banks didn't seem to notice when the three engineers moved away from the table. Gill went over to the internal com unit by the door. He picked up the headset and placed a direct call to the infirmary.

'Is Hallow there?' he asked.

'He's doing a pre-pregnancy clinic with the

colonists. I'm afraid he can't be disturbed.'

'This is urgent,' Gill explained. 'There's something wrong with Banks . . .'

Banks pushed aside the now empty bowls. He found that only Madison remained at the table with him. He felt marginally better but as he looked around the room he saw Tory backed into a corner staring at him and he noticed the other occupants of the Mess, some five or so men and two women were all watching him in wary silence.

'What's the matter with you all?' he yelled. 'Never seen a hungry person before?'

'Banks. You need to remain calm,' Madison said.

'You have nice eyes,' Banks said. 'I never noticed how blue they were before.'

'Thank you. Do you want some more food?'

Madison pushed a bowl of stew across the table. Banks stared at it for a moment as though confused, then lifted the bowl up and tipped it into his mouth.

A few minutes later a medical team arrived. Madison noted that they were all wearing biohazard suits. She glanced around the Mess as the implication slowly dawned on the others there.

'Shit!' said Gill. 'You guys are supposed to have already quarantined him.'

'We did,' said Hallow inside one of the suits. 'Did he touch any of you?'

Banks looked up at the men.

'Come with us Banks,' said Evans. 'We need to give you another medical.'

'I'm fine, Doc. Really . . . I don't want to go back to the infirmary.'

Two of the men in the suits flanked Banks, while a third went behind him. Banks became agitated. He pushed back from the table and stood. He noted how Madison remained seated. She was pretending not to be spooked, but Banks could see the fear in her eyes and that girl, Tory, stank of it. The smell was delicious and it made him feel hungry again. He turned and focused his eyes on Tory. Fresh meat. A sweet little girl. Why hadn't he noticed before how innocent she was? Banks knew he wanted to taste her. The feeling confused him. Something quivered in his brain and he was torn between food hunger and lust.

He suddenly felt something in his mouth. Thin, worm-like, wriggling. Then there were more. Banks began to chew on whatever was in his mouth to break down the suffocating urge to spit them out. They tasted sour and alien.

'Antibiotics. That's all you need Banks. I reckon you just have an infection. Will you let me check out that wound?' Evans said beside him.

Banks glanced down at his hand. It was throbbing and burning again but the scar was almost gone and there was no sign of infection. He opened his mouth to explain. A torrent of maggot-sized worms and yellow ichor fell from his lips and tumbled onto the table. Those that were not mashed and chewed writhed and moved, before slowing and crumbling to a fine yellow dust.

Madison jumped up from her chair as the things fell from Banks' mouth and hurled herself back against the wall but she was trapped between the table and Banks and had nowhere to go.

'My God!' said Hallow. 'Get hold of him.'

Banks was choking on worms now. They were breeding in his throat, in his nostrils; he was even sure they were in his ears. He had to purge.

Madison cringed back against the wall. She was breathing heavily through her mouth as Banks staggered towards her, pulling himself free from the medics on either side of him.

'A kiss,' he said through another torrent of creatures. 'One little kiss. It's all it takes.'

Madison gasped and turned her face into the wall as Banks leaned over the table towards her. At that moment Evans and the two other medical techs caught hold of Banks and pulled him back. His mouth was open and suddenly a surge of bloody ichor and worms sprayed out into the room. By that time most of the people, with the exception of Madison were out of range, but Tory screamed as a gout of the things landed on her shoes. She jumped back yelling, but the creatures writhed and disintegrated just like the previous batch.

'Cover his mouth,' Hallow yelled.

Evans wrapped his suit-covered arm around Banks' throat and pulled him backwards and down onto the floor. Hallow hurried forward, a pressure-syringe now in hand and he plunged the device down onto the side of Banks' neck. He pressed the trigger. A large dose of anaesthetic was injected directly into Banks' blood stream. Banks bucked and fought, but the four men held him down while the drug took effect.

'It's not working,' yelled Evans. He squeezed Banks' throat as more of the vile creatures poured from his gasping mouth.

Hallow placed the syringe back against Banks' neck and fired again. Another dose poured into him. Banks squirmed and fought but after a few moments his struggles ceased as the drug finally began to work and his strength evaporated.

'Someone call this in to the Bridge,' Hallow said as he pulled himself back up onto to his feet. Gill was still by the com but he was frozen with shock.

'Gill!' hissed Madison. 'For God's sake call the Captain.'

*   *   *

Crichton was still manning the Bridge when the call came in. He tried the Captain's quarters but there was no answer and so he

64

authorised the containment of Banks and the people present in the Mess. Then he took a private call from Hallow's office in the medical wing.

'The Mess will have to be stripped down and sterilised,' he said to Hallow. 'All personnel not wearing protection are to be quarantined. What have you learnt so far?'

'Not much. I'm just about to start running some tests on the samples of dust we took from the Mess. We've had to quarantine most of the engineering staff,' Hallow pointed out. 'We have to make sure they haven't been contaminated. It will mean we'll be down to a skeleton crew if there are any issues. And our best engineer amongst them.'

'Better than the alternative. What the hell went wrong Hallow? I thought you checked Banks.'

'We did. Nothing showed up. All of the tests were clear. When he left the infirmary he seemed . . . fine.'

'Okay. We need to see who he came in contact with and get them over to quarantine as well. I'm going to try and locate the Captain, then I'm coming down there and I want a full report.'

Crichton put down the receiver on the Bridge phone as he turned to Dirk. 'I want you to get Third Mate Grisham up here to take over navigation.'

A few minutes later Grisham arrived and

Crichton explained what had happened. 'When you find Fence, tell him to meet me in medical.'

Crichton entered the lift and pressed the level three button. He felt the slightly dizzying movement of the high speed drop. Then the doors opened again and he walked down the short corridor to quarantine. Inside he found Evans and Hallow waiting for him.

'Well?' asked Crichton.

'Banks is in the scanner. Something is wrong with him.' Hallow said.

'Show me,' said Crichton and he followed Hallow into the small observation cubicle off the scanner room.

Under the scanner was a large coffin-shaped clear-plastic box. The box was stood on the scanner table and inside, Banks lay naked with only a thin sheet over his bottom half. A beam of light ran slowly over his body.

'We've scanned him once already . . .' Evans said.

'What did you learn?'

Hallow pointed to the monitor. Crichton could see Banks' body shape, but also all the fine lines and organs that the scanner was reading. At first there seemed to be nothing obvious, but once the beam started filtering over Banks' skull and moved downwards, Crichton saw something very strange. What at first appeared to be brain matter, squirmed and moved like a hive of live insects.

'My God! What *is* that?' Crichton asked.

'Parasites of some sort,' Hallow answered. 'It seems they are eating him from the inside out. His body is turning rotten. It's not surprising he wanted food. These things are consuming him and they started with any areas of body fat. He was clearly trying to replace it.'

Oddly, the parasites weren't feeding on the man's brain matter though. They were in some kind of strange tousle, like some insectile struggle was taking place for dominance and power. The losers among them were consumed by the victors. It was the most grotesque, yet fascinating thing that Hallow had ever seen.

'How has he even been able to function?' Crichton asked.

'We don't know. It's difficult to learn more about the life-form in its transformed state. As I said I took a sample of the dust remaining from the creatures. After a very quick experiment I learnt that blood makes them form into those . . . those worm things . . . It would explain how Banks became infected in the first place. However, when they are exposed to the air they completely disintegrate again.'

'At least, now, we know how to kill them,' Crichton said.

'Well, "kill" might not be the right word really. Change form is perhaps closest?' Hallow said. 'They are clearly some kind of virulent infection though.'

67

'How are the others?' asked Crichton.

'So far,' said Evans. 'Everyone from the Mess seems unaffected.'

'So did Banks,' said Crichton. 'At first . . .'

7

Procreate

Captain Fence didn't remember returning to his quarters, nor did he recall anything after he had entered Sasha's apartment. He felt slightly queasy and an uneasy feeling roiled around in his stomach that had more to do with anxiety than illness. He had been interested in Sasha for a while, but hadn't wanted to make any moves too soon into the journey. It was commonly thought that any bonds made were meant to be permanent, with a view to the future, and Fence had wanted to be sure of Sasha.

One of his concerns had been that she was twelve years younger than him. Fence had always believed that girls that age should gather experience before settling down. That was before things went wrong in the old world and the equation changed. Sexual equality only meant something if you were fertile. Barren men and women were unimportant in the scheme of things. But Fence liked Sasha.

She seemed mature for her years and she always worked well. He couldn't deny that the flirtation he'd had with her was definitely leading somewhere.

He pulled himself up and swung his legs over the edge of the bed. The room was spinning. He wondered if he had drunk too much. He remembered a glass of cheap wine, but couldn't remember drinking any. His head fell in his hands. There was a horrible, murky taste in his mouth, like stale cigarettes, the thought of which made him crave one. But all of those bad things were off limits for the crew and colonists. Keeping healthy, with the occasional alcoholic beverage allowed, was the focus of their responsibility to the new world.

Fence rubbed his eyes. They were sore and tired, but overall, despite a pounding headache, he didn't feel too bad. He stood. He was steady and the room wasn't moving around him. *Good sign.*

'Lights on dim,' he said and the lights in his room slowly faded upwards until his eyes adjusted to them.

He swayed over to the kitchen area and poured some drinking water into a glass. The water tasted odd but he made himself finish it. His headache diminished and he started to feel more like himself. *Perhaps I'm dehydrated?*

In the dim light he could see a message light flashing on his desk. He refilled his glass, opened the medicine cabinet, took out a bottle of painkillers and swallowed two of them. After that he walked over to his desk and looked down at the com. He pressed the button as he sat down at his terminal.

'Captain, this is Crichton. We've had an incident. I need you to come over to medical as soon as possible.'

Another message followed. This one from the Bridge, it was Dirk asking him to go to medical.

The thought of going to the medical area worried him suddenly and he couldn't understand why. His mind probed at the thought of the previous evening. Sasha . . . yes he was in her room. He remembered her stroking his arm, then finally accepting that drink. His mind stumbled again. *God what the hell was that stuff? Some kind of black market moonshine?*

He tried to clear his head but the hangover fugue wouldn't leave. He had to get his act together and call Crichton back. What crisis this time? He sank back into his chair. It was probably another accident, related to some engineering issue. *Again.* He thought about Madison Whitehawk; she had come recommended, but he couldn't help but wonder if she had got the job as Chief Engineer because of her fertility status rather than her ability. There certainly appeared to be no end of problems.

Fence closed his eyes. He had a flashback of Sasha placing her head on his shoulder as they watched a movie together. He hoped that his brief memory loss wasn't some psychotic episode induced by his guilt over leaving Elise behind. His eyes fell on the digital photograph on his desk. Elise's image was there to remind him of his own cowardice and fear.

Sasha looked a lot like her. He knew that was what the main attraction was. A slightly younger version of his wife, only this one could produce the offspring humanity needed.

Fence pinched the bridge of his nose. He felt something warm run from one of his nostrils.

'Fuck!' he opened the top drawer in his desk and tore away two tissues from the dispenser inside. He pressed the tissue to his nose and they came away bloody.

At that moment his com buzzed. Fence jumped at the sudden noise and reached for the earpiece, placing it over his right ear.

'Yes,' he said.

'Captain? We've been trying to reach you! It's Hallow here. We need you down in medical. There's been some form of outbreak. At least, one suffering and we have others in quarantine.'

'*Outbreak?*'

'Yes, Sir. Banks picked something up from the meteoroid. He might have passed it on to Townsend. Apparently one of the crew saw her

71

going into his room two nights ago.'

'Townsend? You mean, *Sasha*?'

'Yes, Sir. We haven't found her yet though, so we're not sure.'

'She isn't in her cabin?'

'No, Sir. But we have a team looking for her. You were on the Bridge with her yesterday. Was she acting strange at all?'

'No. Completely normal.'

'Can you come down here? We need to show you this thing,' Hallow said.

'I'm in the middle of something. There is no immediate danger to the crew and colonists I assume?'

'I don't think so. We think we have it contained.'

'Good work,' said Fence. 'Send me a report and I'll be over there as soon as I can.'

Fence slowly removed the earpiece as Hallow hung up. He felt a strange sense of betrayal and disappointment. Had Sasha spent the night with Banks, before she invited him back to her room? His head hurt. What had happened between them? It crossed his mind that he really should go to medical and get checked out. He had, after all, been in close proximity to the girl. He sipped the water again. It settled down better this time and he felt that the medication was kicking in.

He made the decision and stood up. He would dress and go down to medical right away. He had a responsibility to his crew and he couldn't risk the colonists under any circumstances. A stint in quarantine would be the best thing. And when they found Sasha he would have to ask her all kinds of personal questions.

As he reached the door, there was a knock as though someone had been waiting for this precise moment to let him know they were there.

He opened the door to find Sasha there. She was wearing a long white robe and carrying a bottle of champagne and two glasses.

'I had to go to great lengths to get this,' she said.

Fence stared at her.

'What's wrong? You told me to come. Have you changed your mind?'

'Sasha . . .'

Sasha looked down the corridor. 'Someone could come any minute. Or are you ready to declare us public. Only I'm not sure that's a good idea yet . . .'

Fence stepped back because he didn't know what else to do. He thought perhaps that he should call for hazard to come and take her. But that would be easier if he lulled her into a false sense of security.

'Good job we both have the day off,' Fence said.

Sasha opened the bottle and tipped the frothing wine rapidly into the two glasses. Fence watched her walk towards him, hips swaying. He knew that she was being deliberately provocative.

'To us,' she said holding out the glass.

She had a lovely smile. It was natural and sexy. Fence found it hard to concentrate on anything else. She looked beautiful and alluring. He couldn't help feeling that intense attraction again.

'I still have a hangover from last night,' said Fence.

'You're a bit of a lightweight. You fell asleep after two glasses,' she said.

'I did?'

'Yes. Then when you woke, you said, "Come to my room tomorrow". I was a bit worried about you. You stumbled over to the door like you were still asleep.'

Fence sighed. 'So we didn't . . .?'

Sasha laughed. 'I would hope you would remember if we had.'

Sasha sat down on the sofa and patted the seat beside her. 'Join me?'

'I need to ask you something first.'

She looked up at him with clear green healthy eyes. 'Yes, Captain. That sounds very serious.'

'What is your relationship with Banks?'

'Banks? Why would you ask me about *him*? I thought we covered this yesterday . . .'

'You seem . . . fairly close. If we are . . .' Fence hesitated.

'You want to know if I'll be faithful to you?'

74

'Well . . . yes.'

Sasha placed her glass down on a table beside the sofa. 'Why do you think I'm here?'

'I . . .'

'Isn't it obvious to you?'

Fence felt his heart ache as she looked up at him. She didn't look sick. If she had been infected by Banks then surely she would be exhibiting some of the symptoms?

Fence slid down into the seat beside her. He wanted to love her, wanted to pair with her. Maybe the moment really was right?

He pulled her to him. She smelt of fresh soap and strawberry scented shampoo. He inhaled her. Felt her arms go around him as she drew him down into her arms.

'Our first kiss,' she murmured pressing warm lips against his throat and then moving them over his neck in a hot trail up his chin.

Fence pushed Sasha back and looked into her eyes. He wasn't sure what he was looking for, but what he saw was desire, warmth, perhaps even the beginnings of love. He pulled her to him, closing his eyes as her lips pressed against his and he felt the now familiar exchange that he had begun to enjoy despite his original revulsion.

Quarantine

'Seriously Hallow, you've got to be shitting me. How long do you expect us to stay here?' asked Madison.

'About a week. It took that long for Banks to start to exhibit symptoms.'

Madison stared through the glass. Hallow was on the other side. Madison's lips were set in a grim line. She wasn't happy but she had no choice and would have to accept this if she wanted to get out of here. Besides, if Banks was *that* contagious, she would rather be monitored in the hope that the medics could do something to cure them. Hallow thought this was the safest way of keeping the infection contained if it had spread to anyone else and at least she wasn't in this alone.

'Did you find out anything from the samples of dust those things turned into?' Madison asked.

'It seems that something happened to it when it connected with Banks' blood.'

'Like what?'

Hallow shrugged, he was under orders not to tell the engineers anything more.

'Please, Doc. Tell me what you know. This is scaring the shit out of me. I don't think there's anything wrong with me but it might help if I knew the symptoms.'

'I'll let you know everything when I can,' Hallow said.

'How's Banks?'

Hallow said nothing.

'Shit. He's *dead* isn't he?'

Hallow bowed his head. 'All I can tell you is, this thing . . . this bacteria . . . it's parasitical. It eats away at the body until it has to find a new host. How it passes to another I don't know, but Banks was definitely trying to pass it.'

'Has anyone else got symptoms? Just tell me that?'

'Not so far.'

'That's a good sign then,' Madison said.

Hallow nodded. 'Definitely. We'll keep you in the loop. I promise.'

Hallow left Madison and made his way to the mortuary. This was the first time they had used the room and Banks' body was being contained in a sealed unit. All staff handling him had to wear protection.

'Would you like to say a few words, Doc?' asked Evans as they stood over the coffin.

'No. Just dispose of it. It's looking good for everyone else at the moment. I don't see any need for us to get too carried away.'

The two men stood silently as Evans pressed the release button and they sent the coffin out into the airlock, but both were lost in their own thoughts. Though he said nothing Evans was wondering if Banks had believed in anything before he died. He liked to think he had.

'Good,' said Hallow as the coffin was ejected. He felt an overwhelming sense of relief that the body, and any possible contamination, would now be far from them.

9

Dreams

Madison was floating in an antigravity chamber. She felt happy and free. The feeling of weightlessness untied her thoughts and worries as she drifted over to the portal at the top of the chamber. Outside she could see blue sky above a green and perfect landscape that included flat land nearby and rolling hills in the distance. Aside from the greenery the scenery was reminiscent of the view she had in the Rockies. But she knew this wasn't Colorado, the place of her birth, because that world was no longer beautiful and clean. The mountains long since destroyed by human effort to level the land and make it more habitable. In the end though, they had only succeeded in ruining everything that was good about their planet.

'We made it! We're on New Earth,' Madison said. 'But why am I in here?'

She turned around and looked over to the exit door of the chamber. No one was waiting at the door for her and the com system was quiet.

'Hello? Guys?'

There was no answer. But Madison wasn't afraid or concerned. She could leave the chamber at any time. For now she was happy looking outside at the view.

Can they breathe the air outside? It looked as though they could but she really wasn't sure. She remembered something then, about how the colonists were terra-forming the planet. It would take years to grow all of the plant life that would produce the oxygen they needed to breathe. So, for all the beauty she saw, Madison knew that the air was still poison. Maybe it would remain so for the whole of her lifetime.

The com system buzzed. Madison looked over her shoulder and then a loud bang echoed through the hull and the portal window vibrated next to her.

Banks was looking in at her.

Madison propelled herself backwards and away from the portal with so much force she crashed back into the other side of the chamber before she could stop herself.

Banks' face was a bloated mass. Purple and bruised looking and more of those vile things wriggled from his mouth, eyes and nose. He raised his hand and smashed his fist against the glass.

'No Banks!' she yelled. 'We can't breathe the air. You'll kill us all!'

But Banks didn't care. 'One kiss. One little kiss and you'll feel like I do,' he said.

Madison pushed herself away from the wall. She scrambled along until she reached the hand rails and then she began to pull herself downwards towards the exit door.

'Help! Let me out of here!' she yelled.

She saw Priddy on the other side of the door but his face looked wrong. His skin was yellowed and his nose was bleeding. His bloodshot eyes stared with malevolence through the glass panel of the door.

'Oh my God, Priddy. Not you too?'

Priddy began to hit the door as though he had forgotten how to open it. The bangs echoed around the chamber: Banks hammered on the window, and Priddy continued to attack the door. Madison felt a damp trickle on her neck, and a gout of blood spurted out of her nose. She watched the trail of red liquid float up towards the ceiling of the chamber and spread above her head in tiny weightless droplets.

She placed her hand over her nostrils to try to staunch the flow. Something wriggled inside her ear. Madison turned her head in time to see a thin transparent worm floating beside her.

She screamed, gagging on the creatures as

they filled the inside of her mouth until they burst out into the weightless chamber.

*   *   *

Madison jerked awake with a half gasp, half cry. She looked around confused and then realised that she was still in quarantine. She pulled herself up into a sitting position and looked around the room to reassure herself that she was no longer asleep.

The small glass-panelled room was lined with thin plastic sheeting to buffer the momentary opening of the door to the decontamination cubicle attached to the room. It was obvious that Hallow was taking no chances at all.

One day in this place and I'm already having nightmares, she thought.

The room was lit by a faint red light that ran in a line around the middle of the walls. It was like a night light and it kept the room from being pitch black.

'Lights on.'

The room lit up in its stark white glory. Never had she seen a more impersonal bedroom, but then the sick usually don't care much for special details in their surroundings.

'You okay, Madison?' asked a female voice through the com system.

'Bad dream. I'll get over it.'

'It's Darlene here. Would you like

81

something to help you sleep? I have the Doctor's permission to administer medication if you need it.'

'Hey, Darlene. No, I'm fine. It was nothing really.'

A loud banging noise echoed through the speaker.

'What the hell . . . ?' said Darlene.

'Darlene? You okay?' asked Madison.

'Yes. There's a noise and it seems to be coming from outside . . .'

Madison's heart began to pound as the noise continued.

'I'll call this in. Probably some kind of space trash that's caught up on the grilles. Be right back.'

The com turned off and the sound stopped. Madison looked around the room trying to work out exactly where this room was in the layout of the ship. She was somewhere on the fifth level. This room wasn't against an exterior wall. The thought made her feel strangely claustrophobic.

She pushed back the covers and slipped out of the bed. The *en-suite* bathroom door was to her left. Inside she poured a glass of water from the drinking tap, then filled the sink with warm water. She swilled the water over her face and dried it with a paper towel.

Her throat was dry from the sterile air and so she sipped the drinking water. Quarantine certainly felt different from any other part of the ship. The air used inside the units was not recycled and the fresh oxygen made her feel slightly light headed.

'Darlene?' she called as she went back into her room. Darlene didn't respond. Madison shrugged and climbed back into the bed. Tiredness overcame her previous panic and phobia following the nightmare. She closed her eyes, dimmed the lights and slept.

* * *

Tory wasn't tired. She was upset. Her mind replayed the whole scenario of Banks freaking out. *What were those maggot things?* The whole day had gone haywire and she wasn't at all sure she felt comfortable being prodded and poked by Doctor Hallow and his medical team.

She turned over in the bed. The darkness of the room, coupled with the weirdness of the day, was emphasising every sound. Her room was to the left of Madison's, though Tory didn't realise it, and she was fortunate enough to have a window to the outside. Not that this made much difference: the plastic sheeting covered it, and everything outside was pitch black anyway. There weren't even any stars.

Tory shifted restlessly again. How was she supposed to sleep with all that *banging*?

She heard the airlock for the decontamination tunnel attached to her room open. She turned the lights up and looked at the plastic sheeting across the door. The airlock closed with a thunk and the air hissed inside as the inner door that led directly into her room slid open.

Maybe I'll finally get some answers. Or maybe it's more blood tests. Urgh.

A figure stood behind the plastic sheeting as the door slid shut. Tory thought it was a man but she wasn't certain because the hazard suits made everyone look the same square shape.

'What's all the noise?' she said.

The figure didn't answer.

She pulled the thin covers up to her chin and stared at the plastic curtain. A hand reached out and pushed the plastic away. Tory studied the helmet but the wearer was too far away and she couldn't see who was inside.

'What's wrong? Who's in there?' she asked again.

The man drew closer; Tory could see that the face panel on his suit was steamed up.

'You scared me. Is there something wrong with your com?'

The figure nodded. Tory looked into the panel, the condensation was clearing a little. There was something different about the man's eyes. They were like empty black pits. She didn't recognise them as belonging to anyone she knew. *It's definitely a man*, she thought.

The figure lifted his hands. He twisted the helmet, releasing the top with one practised swing.

'I suppose this means I'm not infected?' Tory tried to laugh, but she slid towards the opposite side of the bed as far away from the figure as possible.

Before he removed his helmet, Tory heard the ship's red alert sound. The man paused, looked towards the door, and then headed back to the airlock.

Once the door closed behind him, Tory expelled the breath she had been holding. She felt overwhelmed. It took her a minute to realise that her heart was pounding. The blood was racing so fast through her body she could hear it rushing in her ears. *I'm scared*, she realised. *Who the fuck was that*?

She couldn't move. She sat with the covers pulled tightly around her.

The red alert light continued to flash, but the noise of the alarm had now been turned off. Tory pressed the nurse call button and waited.

'Tory? Are you all right?' asked Darlene over the com.

'I just wondered what the red alert was.'

'A computer error,' Darlene explained.

'What do you mean?'

'One of the computers registered an external airlock breach. It's not possible of course. So it was probably a wiring error.'

'Has the airlock been checked?' Tory asked.

'Of course. Everything's fine. Go back to

sleep.'

'Darlene?'

'Yes?'

'A man came in here. I couldn't see who it was.'

There was a pause.

'That's impossible,' said Darlene's voice.

'No. Really. Someone came in through the airlock.'

'Go back to sleep,' Darlene said. 'I think you were dreaming.'

'But Darlene, I saw . . .'

'Tory. Honestly. I've been monitoring you all evening. No one has been in there. I'm only outside and no one has passed me. You were sleeping. It was just a dream. I'm sending a dose of relaxant into the air. It will help you go back to sleep.'

Tory looked at the plastic sheeting. It was caught in the door jam, yanked back, exposing the airlock entrance. She was certain she hadn't been dreaming. It was too real, too vivid, and somehow she couldn't help thinking she'd had a lucky escape.

The air-conditioning made a woofing sound and she smelt the chemical relaxant on the air. She tried to hold her breath, afraid to sleep in case the man returned. The air filled with warmth and despite herself Tory's lungs objected. She breathed in the lavender scent as though she could breathe in sleep.

Soon Tory wasn't scared anymore.

As Tory drifted to sleep, she thought she saw movement behind the observation panel, but she couldn't keep her eyes open long enough to make out the figure. She dreamt that it was a man in a hazard suit. As her eyes closed for the final time, Tory's dreams were filled with images of black, burning eyes and a bloated, frightening face hidden behind a visor.

*　　*　　*

Gill was reading a book on his digireader when the red alert alarm sounded. He looked up at the flashing light on the wall above the door, half covered by the plastic sheeting. The alarm itself was silenced almost immediately but the warning light continued to flash. He went over to the door, lifted the plastic, and looked through the glass panel down the shallow decontamination tunnel and through into the quarantine reception. He could see Darlene answering her phone. Then she stood up and walked out of sight. He assumed she had gone out onto the corridor of level five to see what the fuss was about.

Before he had signed up for the trip, Gill had a side-line in safe cracking. It was the family business after all. The sound of the alarm made Gill think of his father. To the outside world Anthony Gill ran a security firm and they specialised in the most secure alarm systems. Gill had a flash of memory, back to the day when he first learnt that his father was not what he seemed. He had been twelve at the time, and he knew enough about electronics to recognise that his father was fitting a trip switch on his latest client's alarm system.

'Shhh . . .' his dad had winked at him. 'You're a smart boy. One day you're going to make me proud.'

Gill *was* smart and he had enough common sense not to ask questions at that time. That evening, Gill senior gave his son his first beer. They sat on the front porch looking out over the street.

'You have to be savvy about these things,' his dad said. 'It's no good fitting the override, then going back a week later to clean the place out. The first person the cops would question is the man who fitted the alarm.'

Gill learnt that night that his father was a very patient man. He had included a special trip switch in all of his systems that none of his clients knew about. He would sometimes wait years before he made a move on any of the properties.

'The thing is, alarms wear out,' his dad had explained. 'If you wait enough time and then do the job, they never suspect you because your alarm has kept them safe all that time. Then, afterwards, you suggest a new and better system to them. The client pays again for you to install it.'

Gill had rapidly followed in his father's footsteps. As the years passed he became an expert in his field. It was one of the reasons he had earned a place aboard the *Freedom*.

Gill knew level five inside and out. It was where he had applied most of his expertise when he was assigned to fit the locks on the labs. He knew how to override the locks on the quarantine chambers. He had even been involved in the design of the keypad locks for the crews' private quarters. No self-respecting engineer of his calibre would install a system that he didn't know a million ways to get around should he need to. It was a habit that he just couldn't shake, even though he was trying to leave his criminal past behind. It was strange when he considered it though. When he had fitted the locks on the chambers, he had never dreamed he would be one of the people locked up inside.

When Darlene didn't return and the light continued to flash, Gill became nervous. What if the ship was damaged and he was needed? What if the rest of the crew and colonists were abandoning the ship in the life-pods? Was he, and the other engineers, being left behind because they might be contaminated? Gill wasn't prepared to wait around to find out. He knew he wasn't sick, despite the overcautious measures the Doctor had taken to be certain. All he needed to do was open the control panel at the side of the door and he would be out of here in seconds.

Gill looked around for something to use as a tool. Obviously he had been stripped of his clothing and the small wallet of tools he always carried had been taken away with his things. For all he knew his possessions had been burned. His eyes fell on the food tray on the table beside the bed. Darlene had sent it through earlier and it hadn't been collected. There was a hard plastic knife and fork on the tray. Gill picked them up and returned to the door.

He used the edge of the knife to try to turn the first screw but the plastic snapped immediately. Gill looked around the room again. There was nothing else he could use. Damn—why did they give you plastic cutlery? What did they think you were going to do with it?

He shrugged. He had made his mind up now and that meant he had to exhaust all avenues before giving up. Gill pressed the broken edge of the knife once more into one of the other screws. He turned it slowly, testing the resistance until he felt the rivet move. After a few turns he was able to remove it by hand. The other screws proved to be easy and so, he was able to manipulate the panel, turning it until the final screw, the one that had broken the knife in the first place, came loose also.

Gill placed the panel and screws down on

the floor. He glanced through the glass again. Darlene's desk was still unmanned.

Inside the hole Gill looked beyond the wires. *Other people would think about cutting the wires to get out of this locked room,* he thought. The natural failsafe would mean the door would spring open. However, it would also mean that an alarm would go up to notify the Bridge that the quarantine had been breached. Gill knew that he had to avoid that. All he wanted to do was take a look outside and see what was happening. Maybe even get onto Darlene's terminal to read up on what they thought Banks had wrong with him. Fortunately he had installed a simple door override on the system that would cut off the alarm and open both doors in the airlock simultaneously.

Good job you taught me to always have contingencies, Dad, Gill thought, as he carefully reached his hand inside the panel, pushing aside the wires to a small hidden switch that only he knew about.

He tripped the switch. A whoosh of air came into the room as both doors opened. Gill paused in the doorway. If he was caught he would probably be in deep trouble. He could easily activate the mechanism from outside to close the doors, and return when it suited him. But in the meantime, he didn't want Darlene to return and see his room open, and his bed empty.

'When in doubt, do the simple thing,' his dad had always said.

Gill returned to the bed, turned the pillows sideways and threw the covers over the top. Then he shut the lights off, and made his way quietly out into reception. He pressed the close button and stepped aside as the airlock doors shut on both sides.

Outside Gill found the medical reception completely empty. It was technically night time and so the ship had a skeleton night crew manning and monitoring the systems. He found the door to the main corridor wide open, but as he looked outside noticed that no one was around. He wondered where Darlene was. It was strange that she had deserted her post. Any official break would have meant a replacement would take over from her monitoring the patients.

Gill approached Darlene's terminal and then thought better of using it to access sensitive information. If he could make it to engineering he could access everything without any suspicion because he knew exactly how to hack into Doctor Hallow's files from there. No one need ever know. Even so, he opened up Darlene's messages, noting the alarm record and that the Bridge wasn't too concerned by the slight blip that had appeared on the system. When he had reassured himself that nothing serious was happening he moved away from the desk.

Gill left medical and followed the red alert lights towards the lift. He would go to his room first and collect some tools. Then he would make his way down to engineering. At night the corridor lights were dimmed to conserve energy. Gill noted the dark shadows but felt no fear or concern. He didn't believe in monsters or spooks of any sort and he had walked these corridors at night many times.

As he passed one of the research labs he heard the lift arriving at level five and the telltale rush of air as the doors opened. Gill ducked into the doorway of the lab. He heard footsteps head his way. It was certain he would be discovered, but he didn't know what excuse he would give. He cursed himself for not putting the panel back. He could have always claimed the doors opened by themselves, declaring yet another computer glitch. It seemed the ship was plagued with those and it was as likely a story as any.

'All looks fine here,' said a male voice close by. 'Not worth bothering with the quarantine area.'

'True,' said a female voice. Because of the hushed tones of both speakers Gill didn't recognise the voices. He heard them turn away, though, and knew they would be walking towards the airlocks in the other direction.

He dared to look around the corner. The guards were out of sight and so he moved to the lift. Fortunately it was still on the level. He went inside and pressed three. He had never felt so relieved to be heading back to his own quarters. As the lift descended, Gill's relief was only short lived. As the doors opened he found himself face to face with Sasha. She was wearing a long white robe, tied loosely with a belt.

'Hello, Gill,' she said calmly. 'I've been looking for you.'

Gill knew he had been found out. He hung his head, expecting Sasha to call the Bridge and tell them of his escape from quarantine.

Sasha took his hand. Gill looked up. Her skin was burning hot to touch but he felt as though he couldn't pull away. She led him from the lift, down the corridor and towards her own room. He felt as though he had no will of his own. It was as though she had some kind of charismatic power over him. An ability he couldn't recognise as even human. Whatever it was he had no time to analyse it as Sasha pulled him, strangely willing now, towards her room.

Sasha's door was ajar. She drew him inside and her robe opened to reveal her beautiful pert breasts. She lifted his hand and placed it on her skin. His hospital pyjamas were thrown aside as she pulled him down into her bed. She rolled him until she was on top of him. Somehow she had discarded her robe too. Gill thought she had the most beautiful body he had ever seen. And her skin was so white and

94

fine that she seemed to glow in the dim light.

Sasha bent and Gill felt a slight sting. He looked down to see her sucking his nipple. He felt a strange dragging sensation: as though his very soul was being sucked out of him.

'We need to procreate,' she said.

Then Sasha's lips were on his. Her kiss was full, deep and he felt a momentary suffocating sensation as she pushed something into him. He coughed and choked as she pulled away, but soon forgot the sensation. He forgot everything, even the fact that he had illegally left quarantine.

10

Fence's Behaviour

'I always wondered what they got up to at one of these things,' said Madison. 'But now I'm worrying that I don't have anything respectable to wear.'

Ten days had passed and the quarantine period was now over. The two women waited for Darlene to bring out their possessions from the lockers in Quarantine.

'You've been invited to the Captain's soirée?' asked Darlene.

Madison and Tory nodded.

'A reward for all we've been through I

guess,' said Madison.

'I have a couple of dresses. Come back to mine,' said Tory.

'I'll call round later,' said Madison. 'I'll see what I can put together first. I wasn't planning on attending parties onboard. First I have to get down to engineering and check how things have been running in our absence.'

Madison took her things and hurried away.

All Tory wanted to do was use her own shower, lie on her own bed and wear her own clothing again instead of the awful hospital pyjamas.

In her room, Tory found a fruit basket from the Captain and a card with her formal invitation to the soirée. She felt excited that she could attend something like this. She had been seeing a young officer, Carl Gershwin, before the quarantine, but he hadn't committed to anything formal yet. Though a few times they had actually come close to pairing, Tory wasn't sure how he really felt about her. Carl had been to see her though, and expressed a hope that she was well. Tory believed that if he saw her in a more formal setting he might consider her suitable to be his mate. There was no reason why their relationship shouldn't move forward after six months and she felt ready to make that commitment.

She opened her wardrobe and sorted through the few formal dresses she had. She put aside two that she thought Madison would like, and pulled out her favourite: a peach coloured dress in pure satin. It had cost her a whole year's salary, but because she was leaving Earth, Tory had decided to blow all of her carefully saved credits on all of the luxuries she wanted to take with her. What was the point in saving money? They would have a different currency on New Earth and wealth would be measured by their level of employment and the children they produced.

After showering she pulled on the dress and admired herself in the full length mirror on one of the bathroom walls. She felt satisfied that Carl would like it and maybe tonight he would finally take her back to his cabin. She felt a small tingle of excitement at the thought. She really did like Carl. For the first time in her life she was willing to sleep with a man and it would mean total commitment on his part as well as hers.

She walked through the bathroom door and came face to face with Captain Fence.

'Captain?' she said. 'What are you doing here?'

The whites of his eyes were a rheumy yellow, and his pupils were black pits. They were exactly like the eyes she had seen behind the helmet of the hazard suit worn by the man who had entered her quarantine room. He stared at her as though he were seeing her for the first time. Tory felt confused by his scrutiny.

'Tory . . .' He staggered towards her, face blank.

'Lights full on!' she said.

The lights came up as bright as daylight. Fence blinked. Then he smiled, but Tory saw this as more of a leer. It filled her heart with fear.

'Tory. I have come to pair with you,' he said.

Tory's mouth fell open in surprise. 'I don't understand. We haven't . . . you haven't gone through the proper channels . . .'

'All of that is meaningless now,' said Fence. 'We need to reproduce.'

'I . . . Captain. I'm already . . .'

Fence shuffled forward. She wondered about his legs, they didn't seem to be moving right. He looked unsteady and confused. Like a mental patient on medication that was slowly wearing off. As Tory backed away into the bathroom he slammed his hand hard against the door, wedging it open. She was trapped between the small bathroom space and Fence.

'Please . . .' she pleaded. 'I don't want my first time to be like this . . .'

Fence straightened up and looked at her. 'You're a *virgin* Tory? I didn't see that on your medical records . . .'

'Captain!'

'I always thought you were the *nice girl* type though. Don't you want to pair with a Captain, girl?'

98

Tears sprung to Tory's eyes. She didn't know what to say or do. The Captain was the ultimate goal for any ambitious girl. She was keen to be *somebody* in the new world, but she had grown fond of Carl. Thought she may even love him. The thought of being with the Captain for the sake of it horrified her.

'Excuse me, Sir,' Tory said trying to pull herself together. She didn't have the charm or experience to outwit him and there was no way she could force the door closed against him. She was trapped and she didn't know what to do. At nineteen years old, she was the youngest crew member, and had so little experience of men.

Fence swayed in the doorway. It was then that Tory smelt alcohol on his breath and realised that the Captain had been drinking. Maybe he had a problem? One she could use to her own advantage?

'C . . . can . . . we have a drink first? I'm . . . not used . . .'

'Good idea!' said Fence.

He backed out of the doorway and Tory moved round him giving him a wide berth in case he suddenly reached for her.

'I think I have something . . .' she said. She rubbed her teary eyes with the back of her hand and swallowed.

At that moment there was a knock on the main door.

'It's Madison,' Tory said. 'She wanted to

99

borrow something for your soirée . . .'

Fence looked around. 'The soirée is tonight?'

'Yes, Sir.'

'I have to go and get ready,' Fence said.

Tory sighed with relief. The Captain straightened up. He almost managed to walk in a straight line. When he reached the door he opened it to find Madison waiting outside.

'Carry on,' he said.

Madison raised her eyebrows as Fence swayed along the corridor. Then Tory grabbed her hand and pulled her inside.

'What was that all about?' Madison asked.

'I think the Captain has a drink problem. He . . .'

Madison noticed that Tory was trembling. 'My God. Are you all right?'

'No. I thought. Shit. It was him. The man that entered my room. I'm sure of it now. And . . . just now . . . I thought he was going to . . . *rape* me.'

Then she fell into Madison's arms and cried.

*　　　*　　　*

A waiter passed through the room with a tray of canapés, which included caviar and rare cheeses on small, fine biscuits. Champagne flowed freely during the soirée, as did the food. There was no sign of any need to ration all of the good things the stores held—

certainly not for the colonists.

There was an odd tension in the air, despite the outward appearance of leisure and although she stood with several of the other female colonists, Syra felt awkward and nervous.

'I heard a rumour that there was some kind of strange outbreak among the crew,' Lisbeth said.

The other colonists enjoyed gossip, it eased the boredom of their otherwise dull existence. Syra suspected that when she was out of earshot they all talked about her in the same scandalized way. They had good reason to feel that Syra wasn't one of them. She had neither wealth, nor privilege, even though genetically she was every bit their equal.

Syra always felt like the outsider. It hurt a little to know that the other women frequently gathered for coffee mornings that she wasn't invited to.

'Champagne,' said Ben returning with her glass.

'Thank you,' Syra said.

She caught Lisbeth looking at her with contempt and in the same glance noticed the sympathetic looks that the other women gave Ben. They believed he was forced to be with her, but Syra knew that Ben was far more into her, than she was him. She was the one who was forced. She quite literally couldn't stand the man and every moment spent with him made it worse. Syra however knew her role and she would play it. Escaping from Earth was a once in a lifetime opportunity and she had no intention of ruining that now. Even so, she felt tense, irritated and incredibly lonely. Sometimes the thought of her future with these people horrified her more than the idea of being left on Earth to rot.

As Ben became engrossed in a conversation with one of the other men, Syra slipped away from the group and wandered over to the buffet table. She wasn't hungry but she couldn't bear to listen to any more of their mundane conversation. She needed time away from it. All she wanted to do was go back to her own room and curl up on the sofa with one of her books, or listen to the music she loved: classical music from the twentieth century. Of course Ben turned his nose up at the songs she enjoyed the most. Her preferred era was the 1980's. The music and lyrics seemed to mean something then and it was so very different from the disjointed noise of the modern era.

'Hello, Miss,' said a respectful voice behind her.

Syra turned round to see Priddy, Gill and Madison.

'Hello, Dave,' answered Syra.

Priddy blushed. He hadn't been expecting her to remember his name.

Madison elbowed him in the ribs, but Priddy ignored it.

'Can I help you?' Priddy said. 'Carry your plate for you?'

'Good heavens, no,' Syra laughed. 'You're guests here too. I heard about your ordeal. It must have been horrible for you all.'

'It was not so much of an ordeal,' said Madison. 'It was more of an annoyance really.'

'Engineer Whitehawk?' Syra said seeing her for the first time.

Madison was wearing a long dress of blue satin. It clung to her slender figure and her usually scraped back hair was loose over her shoulders. Syra noted that Madison looked very pretty when she was dressed in regular clothing, and she wondered why she hid herself under bulky dungarees most of the time. Although she knew they were regulation she was fairly certain that they didn't have to be several sizes too big.

Madison smiled at Syra. *She's not like all of the other colonists,* she observed.

'So who else is with you?' Syra asked.

Madison introduced the other engineers. Syra noticed how Tory stayed close to Madison and glanced around nervously as though she expected to be accosted at any moment. The girl was dressed the part, but she seemed overwhelmed by the party.

While they talked Madison noted that Crichton was absent. They had been playing coy with each other for so long, she wasn't sure what his real intentions were. Not that

103

Madison cared about intentions or pairing. It was one of those things that everyone on board seemed so obsessed with, yet appeared to be no different in reality to the way dating had always been. The men still thought they called the shots. If a woman gave herself to one of them, then she had to remain faithful even if he turned out to be a complete jerk. Madison wasn't ready for that kind of commitment. She wanted excitement in her life and she was hoping that on New Earth she would find it. Still, Crichton interested her and their flirtation was fun. It was a shame really that they had never had that drink together. She had spent the last week in quarantine wondering where it would have led.

A few minutes later Crichton and Dirk entered.

'Ladies and gentlemen, welcome to the Captain's soirée. Unfortunately, Captain Fence won't be joining us this evening. He is a trifle under the weather.'

'Oh thank god,' said Tory under her breath.

Syra was intrigued. 'You okay?' she asked.

'It's nothing,' Madison said. 'Tory, there's Carl. Maybe you should go and see him?'

Tory smiled gratefully at Madison then she left the group by the table and crossed the room to join Carl Gershwin. As she approached, Gershwin's face lit up.

'You look wonderful!' he said.

Madison couldn't help smiling when she saw

104

Gershwin take Tory's hand. The girl was going to be all right now she was sure of it. But the Captain was another issue. It did seem likely that the Captain had been the man in the suit that visited Tory in quarantine. She hoped the incident had all been a momentary lapse of judgement, but knew it was important to tell Crichton what had happened. For the time being though, Crichton was playing host in the middle of a group of colonists and it would be impossible to talk to him. If there was something wrong with the Captain then she wanted to know about it. This could affect the whole crew and the colonists. She had to speak to Crichton alone but that wasn't going to be easy to arrange.

'Ben, what are you doing?' Syra said.

Madison returned her attention back to the group. She had slowly drifted away in an attempt to get to speak to Crichton. She now saw Ben Walsh, holding Syra's arm as he pulled her away from the engineers.

Priddy was flushed, not with embarrassment this time but with pure rage and it was obvious that he didn't appreciate seeing Syra treated so badly.

Ben said through gritted teeth, 'You're embarrassing me. We took you away from the Ghetto—this is how you repay me!'

'Why? Because I'm actually enjoying some interesting conversation for a change?' Syra said. 'What the hell is *wrong* with you? We're all the same. Every one of us on this ship has been picked to go to the new world for a reason. Don't give me this shit about status. I'm no better than anyone else and neither are you.'

Crichton disentangled himself from the colonists.

'Is everything all right?' he asked.

'I want a lock on my door that he can't enter unless invited,' Syra said. 'I'm not a goddamn possession and I'll speak and mix with whomever I please.'

Crichton was taken aback by the vehemence in her voice. 'I agree with you,' he said much to Syra and Madison's surprise. 'No one should push you around. I will deal with your request immediately.'

'But . . . you can't. She's *my* . . .' stuttered Ben.

'Yes I can. My orders are to keep *all* colonists happy, Mr Walsh. It's obvious to me that we have so far failed Miss Connor. She's not *your* anything. She's her own person. All of you are your own. Maybe you need to ponder that before you lay claim to each other in the new world.'

Ben pushed Crichton aside and hurried away. His face was so full of rage that Madison was concerned about what would happen later.

'I'll speak to the Captain about this,' he muttered as he left.

Crichton shrugged.

106

'Let's get you all some champagne,' he said to the engineers.

Syra pointedly ignored the small group of colonists nearby who were glaring at her while Lisbeth whispered behind her hand.

'Can I stay over here with you?' Syra said.

'Of course,' said Madison.

*   *   *

At the end of the evening, the colonists began to drift away and the Officers' Mess emptied. Madison had enjoyed the experience more than she expected to, yet, other than a brief conversation, she hadn't been able to get to talk to Crichton at all. She had so much to discuss with him about her concerns for the Captain and for Tory.

She hoped he would call her or even better come to her room. Tonight she wanted to thank him for what he had said, but also because she had decided that the time had come to stop playing games. She had seen a side of him that night that made her realise that he was not blindly following orders. He had his own set of values, and strangely they resembled hers far more closely than she had expected.

She left the party after she saw Gershwin and Tory leave. Tory looked happy and it seemed that she was going back to Gershwin's room. This meant she wasn't going to be alone tonight and hopefully, once she bonded with Gershwin, it would mean that the Captain would leave her alone. She hoped so anyway: the girl was clearly very much in love with Gershwin.

As she exited the lift onto the crew deck, Madison experienced a feeling of light headed confusion. She hadn't drunk that much of the champagne, but the head rush was somewhat similar. She stumbled against the wall, then waited a moment for the dizziness to subside.

The corridor was quiet and empty. Most of the crew were in bed at this late hour, or working a nightshift. There was a rush of blood in her ears. Madison straightened up. She was certain that she was sensing something but didn't know what. She had always had this kind of sixth sense.

She looked behind her. The corridor curved around to the right. It wouldn't matter which direction you went in, the whole deck was a circle that led back round if you walked it all. She began to walk forward. The deck swayed under her feet and she felt queasy. Her mind slipped in and out of consciousness as though she were in some kind of daze and she felt confused and disorientated.

She staggered across the landing, caught her stumbling body on the wall opposite, then she followed the corridor round. Her room was only a few feet away, yet Madison feared she wouldn't reach it. Sickness curled in the pit of her stomach even as the awful vertigo brought waves of fear. Her sixth sense was screaming and with every step she took towards her room, her real instinct was to turn and run back to the lift.

What's wrong with me?

As she neared her cabin she saw Gill walking towards her.

'Gill,' she gasped. 'Help me . . .'

Gill caught her as she fell forward. The strange weakness she was feeling overcame her body completely for a few moments and then she found herself at the door of her cabin. Maybe someone had spiked her drink? Not something she would have expected to happen in the Officers' Mess, but it could have happened.

'You have to put your code in. Then I can help you inside,' said Gill.

Madison's fingers felt swollen and clumsy, she reached for the panel, stabbed at the numbers without effect.

'What's your pin numbers,' Gill asked. 'I'll do it for you.'

She tried to think, tried to move her mouth, but the sound wouldn't come out.

'You'll have to release your hold,' Gill said.

Madison lifted her head and looked up. Sasha was standing by the door. She looked different. Younger, stronger but so odd and alien that Madison barely recognised her. Her skin was pale and it glowed in the dull corridor as though she held some inner light. Madison had never seen her look more beautiful, and she felt an overwhelming urge to fall into her arms. It was a sexual feeling; one as a straight woman, she was totally unused to.

She felt the lethargy fall away and her limbs began to function as her mind cleared. She shuddered at the thought of her strange compulsion. She remembered something about Sasha. How there had been some concern about her having contact with Banks and yet nothing conclusive had been decided. Why was that? She didn't recall Hallow explaining that Sasha was in quarantine as well.

'I'm not sick,' said Sasha. 'I didn't need quarantine.'

Madison couldn't remember voicing the thought and as her cognitive skills returned she wondered about the coincidence of Sasha knowing precisely what she was thinking.

'Where have you been?' asked Madison. She could stand freely now and she pushed herself away from Gill. His touch was burning hot and something about him suddenly seemed off. *Why didn't I notice that earlier?*

'We need to help you into your room,' said Gill.

Madison looked at Gill. His skin was glowing too. She knew instinctively that Gill and Sasha were no longer the people they had once been.

110

'What are you?' she asked.

Sasha and Gill exchanged a look.

'Madison, you aren't well, we want to help you inside. Will you invite us in?'

Madison turned to the keypad and began to enter her pin, but she deliberately entered it wrong.

'It won't work,' she said. 'I'd better send for Priddy. He'll know how to fix this . . .'

Gill reached out and typed in the correct pin number.

'There,' he said.

A feeling of suffocation descended on Madison as the door sprang open. She fell forward into the room, landing on all fours. She glanced back over her shoulder at Sasha and Gill as they stood in the doorway. Their skin had become luminous. *This is like Halloween*, Madison thought. *Trick or treat?*

'Don't come in,' she said, some deep instinct making her choose her words carefully. 'I'm fine. I'll be okay now. Don't come in.'

Indeed being inside the room and away from them made her feel better. Gill stepped forward, his foot almost crossing the threshold, but Sasha caught his arm.

'You have to be invited,' said Sasha.

'Why?' he asked.

'I want her to be willing. It will make the transition easier.' Sasha said.

Madison fell forward, her strength and energy finally giving out as Gill and Sasha backed away from the door.

11

Unusual Behaviour

'Syra . . . let me in. This is silly. We both agreed . . . I'm sorry. I was a bit of an ass, but you know what the other colonists are like . . .' Walsh said.

Syra ignored him. She was glad that the door between his apartment and hers had a lock. He knocked on the door and she sighed. Syra closed the bedroom door, passed through the bathroom and entered her lounge. The more doors between them the better. She sat down on the sofa and picked up a book that she had discarded earlier and looked at it without reading. The faint knocking continued until it became annoying.

Syra's phone buzzed. She reached over and rejected the call which sent the caller through to her answer phone. A few seconds later a light began to flash to show there was a message. She tried to ignore it but eventually she couldn't resist. She played the message back to find that, predictably, it was Walsh.

'We've paired, Syra. You know what that means. No one else can be with you. I'm going to report this to the Captain as soon as I can get hold of him . . .'

Syra pressed the delete button cutting off Ben's tirade mid-flow. He was such a bore.

The tapping began again next door. Syra put on some music, loud enough to drown out the sound, and curled up on the sofa. What could the Captain do if she refused to continue her relationship with Walsh? They were on their way to New Earth now no matter what.

She submerged herself in the book, and the music covered the sound of knocking. Soon her eyes began to close. She had drunk a lot more than usual that night and it was late. Not that she was used to the lack of proper days and nights—she was, in fact, counting the days when she could set foot on some form of land again. The thought of daylight, sunshine, a breeze through her hair that wasn't created by an air-conditioning unit, were all the things that kept her going on this tedious trip. Syra could almost feel the warmth of sunlight on her cheeks as she drifted to sleep. The book fell from her fingers and came to rest on the edge of the sofa.

*   *   *

A small sound roused her from her sleep. Syra sat upright on the sofa and her book fell to the floor as she rubbed her eyes.

Her music album had finished. She could no longer hear Ben knocking at her bedroom

113

door. Instead there was a loud rapping on her front door.

Syra sighed. It was probably Ben. Bored with being ignored he was trying to get her to open the front door.

She stood up, stretched and walked over to her terminal. Then she selected the door monitor. For a moment it appeared that the corridor was empty. Then the face of a woman appeared on the screen. Syra hadn't seen her before, but she was wearing the uniform of the engineers. Perhaps something was wrong with the computer running the shower unit again and they wanted to check if hers was working? Even as this thought went through her head, Syra hesitated to open the door. She checked the time. It was after midnight shiptime. Very late to come calling about engineering matters.

As she looked at the woman, Syra experienced a strange sense of discomfort. Maybe it was the monitor: perhaps it needed cleaning. The screen was in colour, but those colours appeared faded and wrong. She thought the face somewhat distorted and bleached out, like a photograph taken at the wrong angle and with too much light.

The woman stepped back and then Gill's face came into view.

'You remember me,' he said. 'I was talking to you at the party tonight.'

Syra's eyes felt heavy. She looked at the monitor and at Gill's eyes. In the dim corridor they seemed to pulse with an unhealthy green light. She stumbled back from the screen. She felt tired again but had an overwhelming urge to open the door and let Gill in.

That will show Ben you don't belong to him, Gill's voice seemed to say inside her head.

'Let me in,' Gill said on the other side of the door. 'Syra . . .'

Syra shook her head. Her feet began to move, one step then another as she staggered like a drunk towards the door. Part of her didn't want to go there but another part, that subliminal primal piece of her brain that craved excitement, screamed at her to take a chance. Still she fought against it. She heard Gill's voice, it promised love, happiness, and a pairing that was by preference not by arrangement. The thought of choice made her pull against the compulsion. If she had any options at all, then Gill wouldn't be it either.

Pain erupted behind her eyes as she tried to resist. Her hand flew to her face. She massaged her forehead, but the pain intensified until she took another step towards the door.

'What are you doing here?' asked a voice.

Syra felt herself suddenly released as though she had been a puppet. She flopped as though her strings had been cut, staggering until she regained her own footing.

She could hear voices coming over the com system and hurried back to the monitor. There she saw Gill and the girl facing one of the security men.

Syra had never thought security was necessary on the ship—after all who would attack any of them on board when they were all trying to save the human race?—but it was another one of those silly rules. The security was supposedly there to protect the colonist community and to stop anyone getting out of line. The ship was a community and policing it was something that was deemed necessary. Syra had often thought that even now, when the old world was dying, the powers-that-be were still trying to control the population.

Now, though, she felt grateful to see the guard outside her room.

'I'll ask you again Sasha, why are you and Gill here?'

Sasha smiled and the security guard's formal stance relaxed.

'Rajeet,' Sasha said. 'Take my hand . . .'

The guard took Sasha's hand. Sasha glanced up at the camera set beside Syra's door.

'Sleep now,' she said and Syra felt suddenly tired as though Sasha were speaking directly to her. 'We'll be back soon. And then you're going to let Gill in, Syra.'

The two engineers and the guard disappeared from the monitor as they moved off down the corridor. Syra's mind felt blank and empty. The only thing she could think about was Sasha's words.

'I'm going to let Gill in,' she whispered and

then she lay down on her sofa and slept.

*   *   *

Darlene switched on her monitor and rebooted her computer terminal. There was no one in medical this late. She wouldn't even be here herself but for the fact that she couldn't sleep and she knew that Doctor Hallow wanted the final report on the engineers who had been quarantined. They were all fit and well so it didn't seem that difficult to prepare the paperwork. The strange thing was that she had this nagging doubt; a weird prickle of memory in the back of her head and it made her feel uneasy.

She sat down at her desk and began to flick through the test files. Whitehawk: clear. Priddy: clear. Ansell: clear. She went through them all one after another and nothing stood out.

Darlene rubbed her eyes. She was tired, but she felt sure she was missing something. She had a scanner report in front of her that showed no problems. She remembered passing the engineers through the scanner. Each of them and then . . .

Darlene shook her head. Being forgetful wasn't a trait she normally had but it had been a hectic day. She shuffled the scans on her screen and then laid them side by side until the monitor was full of the reports. Eight in

117

all. Priddy's fell first. She studied it but quickly pushed it aside, sure that nothing was wrong. Then she waded through the others. When her eyes fell on Gill's report her heart jumped. It was a nervous leap, as though some instinct told her this wasn't all okay. But the report looked fine. Better than fine—it looked . . . *just* like Priddy's in fact.

She discarded all the reports with the exception of Gill's and Priddy's. She placed them side by side on the screen, her eyes darting from one and then to the other. They looked identical. Both men had the same small scar on their left femur: an old injury that showed a broken bone during childhood. Darlene frowned. The chances that they had mutually broken their leg in exactly the same way didn't seem likely. She checked the biological age of the scanned body. It fitted perfectly with Priddy which meant that Gill's scan had somehow been lost or become confused with Priddy's.

Darlene sat back in her chair. She couldn't remember processing Gill.

'How can I have made such a stupid mistake?' she murmured. The scan she had taken from the scanner and used as Gill's was definitely Priddy's.

She thought through the day. Gill had been last to pass through the scan room. She was certain he had lain down on the table, just as everyone else had. But she couldn't remember performing the scan. It was all so vague. And there had been so many distractions. The Captain had been down at some point with Hallow and Crichton. Everyone had been making such a fuss.

She ran her hand over her forehead. How was she going to explain this to Doctor Hallow? Surely he would give her a disciplinary for such carelessness. The only thing she could think to do was to try to cover up her mistake.

She picked up the com on her desk and dialled Gill's cabin. When there was no answer she left a message for him to contact her urgently, though she didn't explain why. As she hung up she stared at the reports again. If the scan had been performed it would still be on the computer and she could generate another report. She was certain that all of the engineers had been fit and well and knew it wasn't such a serious problem, but she could still be in trouble.

Darlene logged out of the terminal and went back into the scan room. She opened up the computer and sure enough there was Gill's scan. It was the last one on the system. She sighed with relief. It was okay. All wasn't lost. Just a click of a button and the results would be analysed, the report automatically sent over to join the others. Doctor Hallow need never know and if Gill contacted her she would just say it was nothing after all.

The report was halfway through before Darlene noticed the anomaly. There was an obvious spike on the readings relating to Gill's brain matter. Darlene wasn't a doctor and wasn't sure what this meant but a warning had highlighted now on the report: a warning that she should have seen before letting Gill out earlier. She pulled up the scan recording, which was captured real-time video that would be processed into hundreds of images for later scrutiny. Darlene fast forwarded the recording over Gill's body and focused on the replay around his brain. As the images unfolded she became aware that the anomaly was more than a minor inconsistency. There was something growing, moving even, and it was attached to Gill's cerebral cortex.

'How did I miss this?' Darlene said.

She reached for the com beside the monitor. At that moment the booth door opened behind her. Gill stood in the doorway.

'Gill! Oh thank God. We have to put you back in quarantine . . .'

She stopped talking and stared at the figure that entered the room behind Gill.

'That's not possible . . .' Darlene said. 'Banks . . . you're dead . . .'

'Yes. He is,' said Gill. 'But Sasha let him back in.'

'Hungry,' said Banks. His mouth opened to reveal a set of rotted teeth as he lurched towards her. Darlene didn't even have the opportunity to scream before those awful jaws clamped down on her throat, crushing her larynx. As blood and flesh were ripped from her, Darlene choked and spluttered, drowning in her own blood.

12

Dead Rising

As soon as Sasha and Gill left, Madison had forced her legs to work. She stood up and slammed her front door shut. To say there was something strange about the other two engineers would have been an understatement but Madison couldn't shape it into anything tangible that she could explore. She had no words to express how afraid she really was. It made her body tremble and her heart hurt as blood pushed through her panic-ridden veins. It was like waking up in the middle of a nightmare only to find that the same nameless horror was there in the dark waiting for you. And this felt like a nightmare, so insane, that she wasn't sure anyone would actually believe her if she tried to explain it

Madison thought back to Banks and his eerie behaviour over a week ago. Banks was dead now and Gill and Sasha were behaving oddly, but definitely not the same. *They* were somehow *predatory*. Whereas Banks had appeared to be simply . . . *falling apart*. She had remembered thinking at the time, when all of those awful things came out of him, that he was rotting from the inside out.

When Madison thought of Sasha though, she was reminded of an old childhood poem: *never smile at a crocodile*. Sasha's smile had been cunning. Her face had been . . .

Madison couldn't quite picture Sasha's face now. She saw in her mind's eye the pretty girl Sasha had always been. She had been shy, pleasant and sweet. Madison didn't recall ever hearing a bad word said about her.

Why am I thinking this?

Madison straightened up. *They are still in my head somehow.* But this was just paranoia and she knew it deep down because as soon as she had escaped them Sasha's control had failed. *Escaped? Let go more like. She let me go, like a tasty morsel she was saving for later.* Ridiculous. She prowled her cabin, unsure what to do. Why hadn't Gill and Sasha come in? It didn't make sense at all. Why had they *really* let her go? Where were they now? Dare she risk going to Crichton's room and telling him all she suspected?

He would have me locked up. She laughed at the thought and it relieved the tension but not the total horror she felt of going outside in the corridor this late when most of the crew and passengers were sleeping.

122

Madison stopped pacing and looked around her room. It felt claustrophobic. She really didn't like the idea of being alone tonight. She was afraid that Gill and Sasha would come back. What had happened to them for God sake? Madison remembered the old-style superstitions and myths passed down to her from her grandmother, but she couldn't accurately apply any of these monsters to the strange creatures her old friends had become. She switched on her monitor and looked through the camera outside her door. It looked as though no one was there, but she remembered how Sasha and Gill had just appeared in front of her door.

Madison placed her head on the door and listened. All was quiet. She thought about calling Crichton on his com, or maybe Priddy, but didn't want to wake them.

Suddenly she was concerned about Priddy and the others. If Gill was infected then one or more of them could be also.

I should just go to bed. All of this will seem better tomorrow. And maybe this was just a prank that Gill and Sasha had set up between them. Of course that didn't explain the strange weakness that had overcome her when they were nearby. What was that? How did it happen?

The word *alien* floated through her head. That at least was more plausible than an ancient superstition that no one seriously believed in. There was still so much they didn't know about the galaxy, wasn't that why Banks had been collecting samples after all? To see if there were any potential threats out there?

She sat down on the edge of her sofa but couldn't relax. All she wanted to do was go to Crichton's room. She hated this feeling of vulnerability. It was against her nature to need help from anyone. *It's only one floor up. I have to talk to him about the Captain anyway.*

Shit!

The Captain had been behaving strangely too. Hadn't he wanted to 'pair' with Tory? Now she thought about it the Captain's appearance in Tory's cabin was very peculiar indeed. Tory had never had any contact with him that Madison knew off. She wasn't on the Bridge roster, though Sasha was. Why then would the Captain suddenly get this urge to settle down with a junior engineer that he didn't even know?

Madison's cheeks flushed. Panic coursed through her in an adrenaline rush.

'Okay. So things are getting seriously fucked up.'

She *had* to see Crichton.

She opened her door cautiously and glanced down the corridor. Her nerves were on edge because she wasn't quite sure what she would find around the next corner. It was then that she realised she was still wearing the party dress. She closed the door again, went to her wardrobe and took out her work overalls. At least this would be more practical. She tossed the dress and the ridiculous heels onto her bed and pulled on her overalls and boots.

As Madison closed the door behind her and hurried down the corridor to the lift, she felt less vulnerable than she had earlier. Around the corner the floor was still empty. Madison could see she had a clear line to the lift, as long as no one came around the other side. She pressed the call button and waited, casting glances either side of her.

The lift doors began to open. Madison turned to face it ready to enter and close them as quickly as she could.

The stench reached her first. It was the most awful thing she had ever smelt and it reminded her of death.

He was standing in the middle of the otherwise empty space. His eyes were glazed, face bloated almost beyond recognition, and his skin was moving, as though something was alive under the surface. If it hadn't been for his name tag across his chest, Madison may not have recognised him. It was Banks.

She leapt backwards on instinct, propelling herself across the corridor until her back bumped against a fire extinguisher that hung from the wall.

Banks' dead eyes focused on her like those of a corpse rising from a watery grave. They were whitened, as though cataracts had grown

125

across them. His mouth began to move in his distorted, blue face, but the only sound she heard was the chomping of his teeth together as he shuffled forward. He moved like a decrepit old man, and yet there was a malevolent intent. He was coming directly towards her.

Madison couldn't speak. Her eyes cast around for a weapon. She couldn't let him touch her and yet she was paralysed with fear. As Banks drew closer, a survival instinct kicked in. Madison became aware of what was digging into her spine and, hoping that Banks was as slow as he appeared, she briefly turned her back, grabbed the extinguisher and yanked it from the wall. She swivelled immediately to face him and held up the make-shift weapon between them.

Banks continued to advance; his lips drawn back in an evil sneer. It crossed her mind that he thought her chances of fighting him were too remote. But this seemed unlikely. She wasn't sure if Banks had any thought at all other than to attack.

Banks threw himself forward in a sudden and swift movement that seemed impossible for his condition. Madison swung and the extinguisher connected with his chest. Banks fell backwards and landed on his back on the corridor floor between Madison and the lift. He flopped on the floor like a fish pulled from water and Madison considered making a break for it. She could easily leap over him. The lift doors began to close. Somehow she had to get there and keep the lift on this floor until she could get inside and away from Banks. She stepped back again, extinguisher in her hands. Then she took a short run and jumped. As her back leg followed the rest of her body, Banks' hand reached up and grabbed it.

She fell to the floor, the extinguisher underneath her, and the wind was knocked from her lungs. She heaved in gulps of air. It hurt so much she felt sick. She tried to get up, but Banks was still holding her ankle and so she rolled onto her back and off the extinguisher, pulling it up and round with her. She kicked out at Banks but the roll was enough to free her from his grasp. Behind her, the lift doors slid closed.

As Banks raised himself up onto his hands and knees Madison pulled back her legs and kicked out at him, hitting him in the face with the heel of her boot. The kick barely registered. Banks was feeling no pain. Madison slid backwards, up into a sitting position, shoulders against the lift doors. She raised the extinguisher and swung it towards Banks. The canister connected with his cheek and jaw. Teeth and black blood sprayed the wall beside her as his face was propelled sideways.

Though her limbs screamed Madison bent her legs under her body, and propelled herself up using the now-closed lift doors as leverage. She heard a rumble as the lift left the floor behind her. Fear and panic of now being trapped here brought another rush of adrenaline fuelled by her strong instinct to live.

Banks crawled forward. His mouth was open, his remaining rotted teeth snapped at her like a rabid fox as she pressed herself back against the lift. She looked down at him, hoping to see something of her old colleague, but could recognise nothing in his dead eyes. She raised the extinguisher. Then, as Banks drew nearer, she brought the full force of her weight down behind the canister. It smashed into his skull. Bits of blood, bone and gore clung to it as she pulled back and lifted again.

A red mist came down over her eyes. It was fuelled by the strength of her will to survive. Madison continued to smash down onto his head until Banks' body collapsed and his head was little more than a bloody pulp.

The canister slipped from her trembling fingers. She looked up and down the corridor wondering why the ruckus hadn't brought other crew members from their rooms.

Her bloodied hand reached out and found the call button. She heard the lift start moving, it hadn't been far, maybe one or two floors above her.

Banks' body was falling into further decay. She couldn't tear her eyes away, even as his corpse sank in on itself, shrivelling like a deflated balloon. Translucent worms bubbled to the surface of his putrefying blood, like rats trying to escape a sinking ship. But as soon as they made contact with the air, they dissolved into that fine yellow powder.

Madison shook her head. Shock settled in even as the adrenaline ran hot through her frayed nerves. He had been dead, hadn't he? That's what they were told. And his body . . . she was certain that Hallow had said it had been cast out into open space. Then how did this happen? Had Hallow *lied*?

The door opened behind her and Madison turned. Her heart leapt in her chest as she came face to face with Crichton. For a moment she hesitated. What if he had changed too?

'Jesus. Is that Banks?' he asked.

13

Who to Trust

Madison took the cup of cocoa from Crichton. She was curled up on his sofa wrapped in a thick blanket but her body wouldn't stop shaking. She felt cold and scared.

'Security and the med team are with the body now,' Crichton said.

He sat down beside her. His expression was serious. Through trembling lips she had stuttered out the whole story of Gill and Sasha and when she finally shared the story of the Captain's behaviour Crichton had sent for Security.

'I don't know what's going on,' he said. 'But I'm not prepared to take any chances. I've had the Captain taken from his quarters and placed in quarantine.'

'Did he argue? Fight? Anything?'

'No. He went meekly. He seemed almost pleased. I've seen some pretty unusual things myself the last few days. This is all so fucked up.'

'What have you seen?' asked Madison.

'I was called in when one of the colonists hit his partner for refusing to have sex with him. She said he was acting strangely and he frightened her. When I interviewed him he was very controlled and apologetic. He told a different story about how she had tried to kiss him and he felt something weird being pushed into his mouth. He spat it out, thought it was a maggot or something, then when she grew agitated he had to slap her to make her calm down.'

'That's very weird . . . it sounds like those things that Banks was coughing out in the Mess.'

Crichton nodded.

'There are more incidents I could tell you about. Worse ones, but none as strange as Banks coming back from the dead. Something

130

is seriously wrong, and I'm not sure what we can do about it. Anyway, Security are now searching the ship for Sasha and Gill. So far they haven't found them.'

'What did Doc Hallow learn from his study of Banks?' Madison asked.

Crichton told her about the parasites. 'Hallow was particularly interested in the worms lodged in his cerebral cortex. It might explain their strange behaviour if Sasha and Gill are also infected in this way.'

Madison sipped the cocoa and gazed across Crichton's room as though she were in a trance.

'It's weird but they seem to have some . . .' she started to say.

'Yes?'

She shook her head. 'It seems crazy. Maybe I imagined it.'

Crichton placed his arm around her shoulders and Madison relaxed against him. She told herself that she didn't need comfort but it felt good to be with Crichton.

After a moment, she continued speaking. 'I felt hypnotised or drugged or something. It was as though they could persuade me to do things.'

Crichton let out a long sigh. Madison didn't know what this meant. She wondered if he were thinking she had lost her mind but she had to continue anyway.

'Then . . . as I fell into my room, I felt their

131

influence lift and I found the strength to fight it. They were trying to get me to *invite* them in. Don't you think that's odd? Like they couldn't enter without permission. But that obviously isn't the case is it? They seem to be able to go anywhere.'

'If they have been affected by something alien, who knows what weird connections it's making with their subconscious. Maybe Sasha and Gill think they are supernatural.'

'That doesn't explain their obvious charisma.'

She rested against his chest and closed her eyes. He stroked her hair. It was comforting and, for the first time in hours, Madison felt safe. Before long her breathing changed and her body drooped as exhaustion finally overcame her.

Once he knew she was asleep, Crichton lifted her, turning her body until her head rested on the sofa cushions. She lifted her feet and curled up drowsily. He pulled the blanket gently until her legs and torso were all covered then he gazed down at her for a moment as he reassured himself that she was comfortable.

Crichton sat down at his terminal and logged into the ship's systems. He checked the Bridge. Then he checked medical. He saw a report from Doctor Hallow that the Captain was checked in. Tests and scans would commence in the morning. All was running well. There seemed to be no immediate issues.

As he looked through the report a message popped up on his screen from Security. Doctor Hallow had rescanned Bank's remains and the body had now been incinerated. Several reports had also come in about strange behaviour from different crew members. They had even received a call from one of the colonists. Crichton glanced down at the transcript. It was from Syra Connor. Gill and Sasha had been there too.

There was a note attached to file. Security reported that Rajeet Sunil hadn't reported in, which corroborated Syra's story that he had met with Gill and Sasha. Perhaps he had even met with foul play.

Crichton glanced over at Madison. She was sleeping soundly. Her story worried him. It did seem far-fetched but Bank's body had appeared from nowhere and Hallow couldn't explain it. Hallow was certain they had ejected it from the ship and Evans had confirmed it. He doubted both men were lying. That meant somehow Banks wasn't dead and had come back inside. The only way that could have happened was if someone opened an airlock for him. He was beginning to believe that the false alarm over a week ago wasn't so false. Someone had opened an airlock, retrieved Banks and had kept him hidden ever since. Who that was, Crichton could only guess.

So many odd things had happened lately and they had all started when Sasha pulled

Banks' helmet off in the airlock. The conduct of the Captain worried him too. Then there was the strange behaviour among crew and colonists. It just didn't add up! For example the 'thing' that Banks had turned into was very different from how Sasha and Gill had been described. They were not rotting, nor were they randomly vomiting the worms. The passing of the infection was deliberate. It was planned. Thought out. Even reasoned. Or at least it seemed so. There didn't appear to be any cohesive pattern, nothing in common that he could put his finger on. Except . . .

Crichton stopped reading. Hallow was a common denominator. When it came down to it, if some of the crew had become contaminated by something that Banks brought in from the meteoroid, then they could all potentially be in danger. Anyone could be infected. How could he know who to trust if they, unlike Banks, appeared to be normal? Or could act normal when they wanted to?

Another message came up on his monitor. Rajeet Sunil had been found and he was fine. Crichton replied with an instruction to quarantine Rajeet anyway.

His mind went back to the problem of Hallow. He needed to go down to medical and check things out for himself. He was even tempted to get the doctor taken into custody. He wasn't quite sure if he should trust Hallow at all.

Crichton turned once more in his seat and gazed at Madison. He couldn't deny he had strong feelings for her. He had been coming to her room to ask her if they could start seeing each other with a view to pairing and he had been glad to learn that when she was frightened she had been trying to get to him. Even so, she was a tough cookie. He had always thought that. What other female on board would have fought off a crazed dead man? He couldn't imagine any of them being so resourceful or even most of the men for that matter. She was one in a million.

He stood up and stretched. He really should go down to medical and maybe take a physical look at the Bridge even though their journey was totally automated and staff were there just to man the controls in the event that something went wrong.

Madison stirred and opened her eyes.

'I need to go and check on something,' Crichton said.

Madison sat up, and pushed aside the blanket. 'Can I come with you? I don't want to be alone.'

*　　　*　　　*

In medical Doctor Hallow was looking through the file containing the scans. It wasn't long before he noticed that Gill's scan wasn't there.

Without knowing it he followed the same pattern as Darlene, and eventually logged into the scanner terminal to see the results. As his fingers tapped on the virtual keyboard that lit up on the desk before the monitor, Hallow felt something sticky beneath his hand. He turned off the keyboard and looked down at the table top. There was a small pool of congealing blood. It looked to be nothing more than a splash, as though someone had a sudden nose bleed and had failed to notice the spillage.

He went out into the reception. There was a guard on duty.

'Where's Darlene?' Hallow asked.

14

Pairing

They gathered in the Officers' Mess on level seven shortly after the red alert was raised and Crichton had ordered a lock down on the Bridge. There was less than a third of the crew remaining and only half of the colonists. The rest were all technically 'missing'. They had sent a team of security men and women out to search the ship, because someone had sabotaged the surveillance equipment, and the missing crew and colonists weren't responding to the com calls. One group reported finding

136

the camera computer 'tampered with', the hard drive had been removed. After that Crichton had ordered a lockdown on all of the computer rooms so that no more damage could be done. He was most concerned about the life support units, but so far the infected mutineers hadn't made any attempt to touch those, nor had they tried to get into the bridge. All of which indicated a level of intelligence that Crichton found reassuring. Maybe they could be reasoned with for the good of all of their survival.

Crichton was glad to see Carl Gershwin and Tory Ansell, plus the colonist Syra Connor among those safely in the Officers' Mess. A few of the colonists had been stubborn but Madison took it on herself to calm them down, leaving Crichton to talk to the remaining crew members.

The Mess was the only single room big enough to accommodate all of the remaining people on board, but it seemed less cramped than it should have. Crew and colonists were spread out into the different areas. The bar area, the relaxation area and the eating area all seemed relatively empty.

Crichton found Hallow sitting by the bar drinking a whiskey.

'You have to tell me everything you know,' Crichton said.

'I've told you all so far,' Hallow said.

The doctor was being unusually surly and

this made it even harder for Crichton to trust him. There were way too many questions left unanswered.

'You must know something. You've examined the infected and you did tests on the meteoroid shard.'

'There are still some tests running in the lab. They may tell us something,' Hallow shrugged.

'Right. Let's go down there and look then shall we?' said Crichton.

*　　　*　　　*

As they exited the lift on level five Crichton had the overwhelming feeling that he was on a ghost ship. Even though technically it was the middle of the night, there were usually crew on duty during this time: technicians monitoring the systems, someone always on the Bridge, and medical was usually manned by at least one nurse in the event of an emergency. There was of course no one around now because everyone they had found was in the Officers' Mess.

As they reached the lab and Hallow opened the door, Crichton left two of the guards with him while he and the other two went into quarantine to check on Captain Fence and Rajeet.

The reception was deserted as expected but they found Fence's quarantine room open. Rajeet Sunil was also missing. Inside one of the rooms Crichton found signs of a struggle. Someone had walked in, opened the booths and taken the men and by the look of it they hadn't gone willingly. Crichton hoped that this meant that Fence and Rajeet hadn't been infected at all.

'Search for them! They can't have gone far.' Crichton said. Even though the whole of the ship had been searched already and it didn't seem rational or possible that they would find them. He just hoped that they would, all he wanted was to save as many of the crew and colonists as possible.

The two guards left Crichton alone as they began to systematically search level five. Crichton looked around reception, opening and closing examination rooms, all of which were empty. He had ordered lockdown on this zone as well as the Bridge. Hallow had been left to do this task and clearly he hadn't done it properly.

At that moment he heard a noise behind him, Crichton turned to find Hallow and one of the guards standing in reception. He hurried towards the door as Hallow came towards the quarantine unit that had contained the captain.

'The lab has been destroyed,' Hallow said. 'I thought this was just paranoia but now . . .'

'The test results? Did they make it onto the computer system?'

Hallow shook his head. 'Where's the

Captain?'

Crichton shrugged. 'I don't know.'

He found that Hallow was blocking the door as he approached the airlock. 'Excuse me?'

'You okay?' asked Hallow.

'Of course I am. Why?'

'Where are the guards?'

'Searching for the Captain of course,' Crichton said. He frowned. 'Let me pass.'

'Not until I know what's going on. What aren't you telling us?' Hallow said. He put his hand over the door lock.

'Hallow, I don't know any more about what's happening than you do. In fact it's you that needs to share what you know. How exactly did you dispose of Banks' body for example?'

'We put it out of the airlock.'

'Who is *we*?'

'Evans . . . and . . . Evans! He *wasn't* at the Officers' Mess!' Hallow said. 'I haven't seen him for several days in fact.'

Crichton pushed Hallow out of the way. 'And it didn't occur to you to mention this to anyone?'

'I assumed he had some leave . . .'

'Okay. Did you see Banks' body immediately prior to expulsion?' Crichton asked.

'Yes. I had to sign it out . . .'

'He was definitely in the casket?'

'Yes! I swear he was.'

'Then how the hell did he reanimate and get back inside?'

'It isn't possible. I know that and I've been wracking my brains.'

There was a sudden commotion behind them and Crichton turned to see that one of the guards was stumbling around, his eyes and nostrils streaming blood. His skin was bleached and his lips had turned blue as though he were cyanosed. The guard clawed at his eyes and then coughed. A cluster of translucent, maggot-like worms shot from his mouth and across the reception area. He bent over and began to vomit more worms from his lips onto the floor where they rapidly disintegrated.

'Grab him!' yelled Crichton, but the other guard backed away as his colleague coughed up squirming horror before his eyes. Crichton hurried forward, grabbed the infected guard by the arm and yanked him towards one of the quarantine rooms.

The guard tumbled and fell down on all fours in the airlock between Medical and the quarantine room. Blinded by the worms seeping from his eyes, nose and mouth, the infected guard began to crawl towards the room as the inner door began to close. He floundered, only half inside the room as Hallow, Crichton and the other guard watched through the glass panel.

'Get into the room,' Crichton said through

the com but the man was behaving as though he had been given lithium. He didn't seem to have full control of his limbs.

He began to heave again as though the awful things inside were choking him. Then he fell forward and dragged himself further into the room. Almost through the door he paused as more of the vile worms spewed from him. Crichton noticed that the man's leg was caught in the rapidly closing pressurised door. Then, as though he became aware of it himself, the guard pulled forward again, but not fast enough. The door began to close trapping the man's leg, just above the knee. He screamed. It was a cry of insane agony.

'Open the door! We can't leave him like that!' said the other guard.

'We can't,' said Hallow. 'Now that closure is reactivated, the door this side won't open while that door is ajar.'

As the door continued to squeeze closed, Crichton turned away and switched off the com cutting off the awful screams.

'But . . . both doors were open when we came in!' protested the guard. 'How did that happen if we can't do it?'

'I don't know! God Damn it! Someone must know of an override . . .' Crichton said, walking towards the reception desk. He couldn't watch the horrific scene unfold. He felt as though he were losing it. There were too many mysteries to solve and too many people still missing for his peace of mind. *Where had they all gone?*

There was a hiss as the airlock pressurised. The inner door had closed leaving the poor man's severed leg inside the airlock. Hallow watched in fascination as it bloated, rotted and rapidly disintegrated.

'There's more to this that I can understand at this time,' Hallow said.

'What do you mean?' Crichton asked.

'I tested the drop of blood I found earlier. It was Darlene's.'

'I thought as much since we couldn't find her.'

'That's not all. She was anaemic,' Hallow said.

'So?'

'No one on board had any health issues. That's why they were picked. Everyone was in peak fitness.'

'Yes. But she maybe . . .' said Crichton.

'No,' interrupted Hallow shaking his head. 'I gave her a medical only last week. The blood tests came back normal. This was something that has happened recently.'

'How recent?'

'I don't know,' said Hallow. 'But possibly as little as twenty four hours.'

'Darlene might be one of them?' Crichton said. 'Is this a symptom of infection?'

'Possibly,' Hallow shrugged. 'I just don't know. And without subjects to test I don't see what else I can learn.'

'What's going on?' asked the guard. 'What happened to Alec?'

Crichton and Hallow ignored him. 'You're making a lot of suppositions without any real evidence to back it up,' Crichton said. 'So what else aren't you telling me?'

'Her blood . . . it was only a small amount you understand . . . a drop.'

Crichton nodded.

'But I can tell you more about *this* condition than any other. I scanned Banks remember,' Hallow continued, nodding towards the quarantine room. 'I discovered those things were all through his body. They were *eating* him from the inside. It was like he was walking food to them. A parasite of the vilest kind. I don't know how it gets passed on though. Touching them doesn't do anything . . . Banks' blood was also low on iron, but not enough to call it anaemia.'

'What are you saying?'

'Earlier today I found this,' Hallow said, logging into the terminal on Darlene's desk. He pulled up the now complete report he had found on Gill. Hallow ran the recorded footage and explained how he had found something lodged inside Gill's brain.

'Gill was released even though Darlene had taken the scan that showed him to be infected. Somehow or other, she sent me a different report. It could mean she was already infected herself by then.'

'What is it?' asked Crichton looking at the scan image. He could see something strange and alien moving within Gill's brain.

'My best guess—it's one of those things. It's connected to the cerebral cortex and it's probably controlling him.'

'Are you telling me that this is an alien life-form capable of controlling a human mind?'

'Maybe controlling was the wrong word. You see it's *joined* with him. It's a kind of pairing. An evolution if you like.'

'Evolution into *what*?' said Crichton.

'An evolution into a hybrid human. This thing does something to the brain, the memories, but I don't know what exactly.'

Hallow fell quiet for a moment and when he began to speak again his words were carefully and slowly delivered, as though he were speaking aloud the ideas as he explored them in his mind.

'The thing I don't get is why this doesn't just happen to all of them. Why do some go like . . .' he glanced over at the quarantine booth containing the guard. 'It's as though the parasites are breeding inside some people, but not others.'

'Give me another best guess,' suggested Crichton.

'I suspect we are dealing with two completely different species. Of course this is only a theory. I won't know for certain until I can get my hands on Gill and Sasha. So far I've only ever examined this kind. But I think that Banks and our guard there are failed pairings. The worms multiply, attempt over and over to find a match, then the body rejects them. Somewhere in the process they try to find another body to merge with.'

'Pairings?' said the guard, suddenly interested in what was being said. 'Like sexual?'

'Kind of, in a way,' Hallow said. 'These things go after the brain in much the same way that a sperm will try to penetrate an ovum. Then a similar reaction occurs. The cells join and begin to multiply, changing each part into one new being.'

Crichton looked towards the quarantine booth. The memory of Banks' awful lips moving towards Madison as he tried to kiss her sent a shudder down his spine. 'Maybe sexual contact is one way to pass it on. Hallow I want you to look through the crew records, see if there is any common denominator between Banks and the guard in there . . . Jesus, what is his name?'

'Alec,' answered the other guard. 'He's Alec Torrenson.'

Hallow nodded and began to access the crews' medical records.

'This could take some time.'

'Time seems to be something we have a little of right now,' Crichton said.

At that moment Torrenson pressed the com

146

from inside his quarantine booth. Crichton, Hallow and the security guard outside looked at each other as Torrenson's horrible laughter echoed around the room as though it were coming from an open grave.

'Shut that thing off,' said Crichton.

'Why is he laughing like that?' asked the other guard.

'He's insane,' Crichton said.

'There is one other thing I should tell you,' Hallow said.

'What's that?'

'The pairings are happening much faster now.'

'What do you mean?'

'At first, the change in Banks took more than a week to happen. I think this was probably due to Banks' natural immunities. But now that the creatures are evolving, they have learnt how our bodies work. They make it to the brain in minutes now, rather than days. I think, and this is only a guess based on some of the tests I've done, that it's learnt to bypass our immune systems. That man in there . . . he was probably only infected a few hours ago.'

*   *   *

'Let's get these people some food,' Madison suggested.

The kitchen was in total darkness which wasn't a surprise because the chefs had retired

147

hours ago once the soirée had ended. Madison switched the lights on and she and Tory entered the kitchen and began to look around. Gershwin had opened the bar and was serving drinks to the colonists while various crew members were taking their turn monitoring the lifts. Others were trying to sleep, but that seemed like a luxury to Madison and she couldn't have switched her mind off if she had wanted to.

'I need to go to the bathroom,' said Lisbeth following them into the kitchen.

Madison glanced back at her. She recognised Lisbeth as one of the least nice of the group of colonists she had mingled with earlier that evening. She recalled that the woman had snubbed her and the other crew members, but she said nothing. It was just the way the colonists had been treated that made them behave like such snobs. Madison knew that when they reached New Earth though, it would be a testing time for them. One which would make or break many of the colonists. That was, of course, if they *ever* made it to the new planet.

'There's one down that corridor,' said Tory. 'It's crew only usually, so you'll have to forgive the basic amenities.'

Lisbeth walked down the corridor until she found the crew toilet cubicle. It was quite a distance from the kitchen area and it felt eerie. She didn't understand what was happening outside but the whole thing with the missing colonists made her feel oddly nervous and scared.

She opened the door and jumped.

'Jesus! You scared me. Sorry for walking in on you.'

Ben Walsh was inside. He was standing still, staring at her. But his face was oddly swollen, tinged with blue.

'Sorry,' she said again, moving to close the door. 'I expect Syra will be glad to see you . . . she's been . . .'

Walsh's hand shot out. He caught hold of the front of her dress and pulled her forward. Lisbeth barely had chance to gasp before Walsh clamped his lips over hers.

*   *   *

As he crawled through the maintenance shaft, Priddy realised that he had never been issued a direct command before from the Captain.

'There is a problem in maintenance shaft two,' the Captain had said.

Priddy had blinked: half asleep he had automatically picked up the com beside his bed as it rang.

'Yes, Sir,' he had mumbled. 'What seems to be the problem?'

'The computer is showing a failure on one of the air filters. It's probably nothing but would you check it out?'

149

He followed the shaft right until he came to the panel that covered the mechanism running the air filter. There was a keypad attached to the panel. Priddy tapped in the passcode and the panel opened. He shut down the filter, diverting its task to a standby machine. Then he studied the motherboard. One of the main wires was burnt through.

'That's odd,' he murmured.

The tunnel was lit by bright white strip lights. Priddy could see well, but he retrieved a small torch from his bag and focused it on the motherboard. The wire was burnt, yes, but there was something else wrong: one of the other feeds was broken. He looked at the edges of the wire. It was a clean cut, as though someone had used wire cutters. The resulting damage wasn't serious, just annoying. A prank and easy to fix. But who would do this and why? More importantly who had access?

He felt an urgent need to talk to Madison. His practical joker days were long over and so this meant someone else was fooling around, but it concerned him that Madison may think he was responsible. And, after what had happened to Syra, he would never behave like that again. Syra had made him realise that not all of the colonists were arrogant.

Priddy repaired the damage, closed the panel and packed away his tools. A few minutes later he was crawling back out of the maintenance shaft. The red alert alarm

150

went up, followed by an announcement for all personnel to come to the Officers' Mess, as he closed the hatch on the shaft. He made his way to the service elevator. As the lift opened Priddy found two security guards inside.

'Is anyone else down here?' one of the guards asked.

'No,' Priddy said. 'What's happening?'

The second guard shrugged, 'We don't know. We have orders to search every floor and bring anyone we find to the Officers' Mess.'

'Ok,' Priddy said. 'Let's go.'

Priddy stepped into the lift. The first guard pressed the button for the next floor up.

'Will you hold the lift while we check this?' the guard began as the doors opened.

It took a moment for them to make sense of what they were seeing. A pile of red clutter lay in the centre of the engineer's deck. It looked as though someone had emptied the meat locker from the Mess kitchen and left it to rot by the lifts. The two guards pulled their stunners from their holsters.

'What the . . . .?'

The gore began to heave and writhe as something moved within it. Priddy could make out the shape of a spine as a body unwound from the foetal position. It was a woman: her bare flesh was smeared with blood. With a shock he realised it was Sasha.

More shapes detached from the bloody

151

mass, among them was Captain Fence, naked as the day he was born. Fence grinned. It was an expression of insanity. His face was a swollen, bruised mass, as though he had been in a serious accident.

'Captain?' said the first guard.

There was a strange feeling in the air, as though someone had suddenly pumped the oxygen with hallucinogenics. Priddy felt dizzy, confused, and as his eyes fell on Sasha, a strange compulsion filled his senses. He wanted to *belong* to her. He shook his head, the image of Syra floated behind his eyes. This was wrong!

He saw that Sasha was naked, and looked beyond her to the pile of bloody bodies. Darlene was in a clinch with Gill, even as her mouth was clamped on the arm of a man. Her throat was a bloody mess, as if someone had tried to eat her. The man lay, eyes open wide in shock, chest heaving.

'Priddy?' said Sasha. She was beside him now, fingers, nails like talons, gripped his arm and he felt his will slip away. He moved from the lift doorway and out into the corridor as she gently pulled his arm. As though they were all attached the two guards walked forward also, flanking his sides.

Some were dead, some very much alive and feasting on the carcasses. Priddy thought he heard music. It drowned out the sound of the Red Alert, and the horrible slurping noises that came from the pile of bodies before him. A primal instinct made him aware that the lift doors were now closing. Priddy felt a momentary panic and then Sasha's hand stroked down his chest and the feeling receded like the half-remembered fragments of a bad dream.

One of the security guards screamed. The sound penetrated the music. The strange apathy began to lift and Priddy became aware of Sasha again. Something malignant sat on her tongue as her mouth opened to place a kiss on Priddy's lips. He pushed her away, his hand automatically reaching for the large spanner in the pocket of his overalls. Sounds and sensations continued to return as Sasha released her grip, Priddy yanked his arm completely free, backing towards the lift. He reached behind him, fingers blindly searching for the call button while his eyes darted around the corridor. One of the guards was being eaten by two men wearing colonist uniforms. The other was fighting for his life as two females tried to place their contaminated kisses on his lips.

Priddy raised his spanner. There was a sound, like a collective gasp, as all of the creatures—he couldn't think of them as his colleagues anymore—stopped what they were doing and turned towards him.

Gill was suddenly there, pulling Sasha backwards until she was cocooned by Fence,

Darlene and several other naked bodies.

The second security guard pulled himself free of the two women. He backed up against the wall, sliding along it as he made his way back to the lift. It was then that Priddy became aware of the alarm again. The music grew louder, but he focused on the alarm and it pushed away the hypnotic sound. Priddy's fingers found the call button. As the door opened, he pulled the remaining guard back into the lift. At that moment Fence rushed forward. Priddy swung the spanner and it connected with the Captain's head.

The man staggered but kept coming. Now that he had drawn first blood, the creatures outside began to howl. There was nothing human in them that he could recognise. Fence fell upon Priddy, teeth snapping towards him like a frenzied animal.

The creatures outside became frantic as the lift doors closed, leaving Priddy, the security guard and Fence inside.

'Get us out of here!' Priddy gasped as he brought the spanner down on the head of the Captain again.

The guard panicked and began to press buttons.

Priddy pushed Fence backwards and as the lift began to move upwards towards the next level, the guard pulled his stunner and fired it at Fence.

The Captain's body jerked, and smashed

back against the lift doors. As Priddy brought down his spanner, smashing open the man's skull, blood and worms spluttered from the wound.

'Stop. He's dead,' said the guard.

Priddy's arm hammered down once more. He looked down to see the bloody pulp that was once the Captain, now sprawled at their feet in the cramped lift.

The guard was shaking from head to foot, stunner still pointed down at the body.

*　　*　　*

'How's this?' said Madison.

Tory looked into the large fridge. They saw the remains of the soirée food carefully laid out on trays, covered with cling wrap.

'That will do nicely.'

Madison found a trolley and they filled the three tiers and wheeled it towards the Mess quarters.

'Haven't seen any of the chefs either,' Tory mentioned.

'I was thinking that too,' Madison said. 'Hopefully they are just conked out in their quarters and didn't hear the alarm.'

Tory said nothing but she moved forward and opened the door to the Officers' Mess while Madison wheeled the food trolley through.

'Wait up!' called Lisbeth behind them. 'I

really don't want to be alone in here.'

Tory stepped back and let Lisbeth pass before she closed the door behind them.

In the eating area some of the crew and colonists stirred to see what they had brought in but Madison noted that several had curled up on the floor or a lucky few had found sofa space in the relaxation area and were sleeping. She pushed the trolley to the corner of the bar and stepped aside to let anyone who wanted food come and help themselves.

'A drink?' Gershwin asked.

'Water please,' said Madison. She wanted to keep her wits about her and they had drunk enough alcohol earlier.

Gershwin poured the water from a jug and then opened a bottle of wine for one of the colonists. It was as though the party was continuing despite the strange circumstances that brought them all back together in this room.

Madison took her glass and went into the relaxation area. She felt tired now and could think of nothing nicer than curling up and going to sleep but there was a heavy tension in the air. She couldn't tell exactly what it was, but she felt that any minute something was going to happen and it wouldn't be nice. She found a corner and sat with her back to the wall and watched the crew and colonists as they ate. As she brought the glass of water to her lips Priddy burst into the room followed by the security guard. The corridor guards came in also and closed the doors behind them.

'Is this okay?' one of the men watching the door asked.

'Of course! We're glad to see these men,' said Gershwin.

'Where's Crichton?' Priddy asked.

Madison put down her untouched drink on the nearest table and stood.

'Where have you been?' she asked.

It was then she noticed that his boiler suit was ripped and discoloured with dark oil-like stains. Madison knew instinctively that this was not engine grease: it was blood. It looked just like the blood that had spurted from Banks when she had hit him with the extinguisher. Priddy was trembling and so was the security man with him.

'What happened?' she asked again.

Priddy sank down into the nearest available chair in the eating area. 'There were . . . the *worm* things?' Madison asked.

Priddy glanced over his shoulder at the guard. 'You should get some water and food.'

'Tory?' Madison called. 'Please help this man.'

The other crew and colonists were becoming curious now and so Madison led Priddy to one side.

'They were monsters. Not even recognisable as human anymore, even though I knew some of them were my colleagues.'

157

Madison felt bile burning the back of her throat as Priddy's spoke. 'Sasha started coming onto me . . . It was so weird . . . I almost felt like I couldn't help myself.'

'Priddy . . . did she touch you? Did she . . .?'

'No . . . I don't know how but I focused on the red alert. I started hearing the alarm over and over, even though it had stopped ringing by then, and something in that gave me the strength to get back into the elevator. I pulled the guard with me. The Captain is dead,' he said. Then in whispered tones he told her of the battle. 'His body is still in the service lift.'

'We're going to be okay, but I'm worried about Crichton now. They've been gone for a while,' Madison said.

'Here's some water,' said Tory holding out a glass to Priddy.

Priddy took it and thanked her but as he raised the glass to his lips, Madison knocked it from his fingers.

'What the . . .?'

'Don't drink!' she cried. 'There's something in the water!'

15

Keeping Command

'I tried to call the Mess but the lines are down,' Crichton said. 'We need to get back up there Doc. I'm worried about those people being left alone.'

Hallow nodded. 'I have everything now. I can analyse it all when we are back with the group. But I can't see any common denominator on why some people would go like . . . Torrenson and Banks and others become controlled like Sasha and Gill. Natural selection maybe?'

Hallow saved the information onto his personal digireader and stowed it in a small bag which he then attached to his waist.

'We need weapons,' one of the other Guards said, having returned from checking the level. 'We have to get into the armoury.'

'You have stunners,' Crichton said, gesturing to the compact stun-pistol holstered on the guard's belt.

'Do you think a stunner would work on him?' asked another guard nodding towards Torrenson's quarantine booth.

Torrenson was leering through the two glass panels into reception: worms poured from every visible orifice. They even fell from his hair like dandruff, and his facial skin squirmed as though the creatures were moving underneath.

'They are everywhere in him now,' Hallow said. 'Under his skin, in his vital organs and they're feasting on him.'

'If that's so,' Crichton said, 'then why did Banks come back from the grave? Why wasn't he just food?'

Hallow said nothing.

'We could try the stunner on him,' Crichton said, 'but I don't much fancy opening up that room.'

The three remaining guards all looked relieved.

'We go to the armoury then?' the first one asked again.

'Yes. But we have to choose carefully. Bullets can't be fired on board, not without risking a hull breech. But I think I know what we can use instead.'

They hurried down the corridor and made their way to the staircase. The armoury was one floor down on level six.

'Let's use the stairs,' Crichton said as one of the guards turned towards the lift.

'Why?' asked Hallow.

'If someone is messing with the com what's to stop them from freezing the lifts too?' Crichton said. 'We have to retain command of the ship and we can't do that if we're trapped in a lift.'

The staircase was in evening mode. Dim emergency lights ran along the walls and across the front of each step.

'This is like a horror movie,' one of the guards complained. 'It's dark and too quiet.'

'Lights on,' said Hallow and the main illumination came on. 'Not quite. Get moving and try not to let your imagination run away with you. Okay?'

Crichton went first with one of the guards, Hallow was in the middle and two more guards brought up the rear. As they reached the next level down, however, the lights went out, plunging them into gloomy darkness.

'It's on a timer,' Crichton commented. 'No need to get jumpy.'

Despite the fact that none of them had been under attack they were all nervous. Crichton likened it in his mind to that prickling sensation of becoming aware that you are being watched. It felt malignant and despite his outward calm he was intimidated by the unknown as much as the guards were. The ship held that *Marie Celeste* feeling of instantaneous emptiness. Crichton couldn't help noticing the absence of noise. And the silence was giving him the creeps. As he opened the door to level six Crichton almost expected to find something sinister waiting for them. But the floor was as empty and deserted as level five had been.

The men stood in the doorway for a moment as though unsure how to proceed.

161

They felt nervous as they looked down the corridor. Then Crichton started to move towards the armoury. They passed several rooms along the way. This level held the greenhouse pod. Fresh fruit and vegetables were being grown as well as wheat and corn in smaller quantities. The seeds of which were harvested and stored for future plantation, while the fresh vegetables were already being used to feed the crew and colonists.

Gardening tools were kept in the room next to the armoury. Both rooms were locked and only those with clearance had access to them. Crichton knew that the armoury hadn't been opened since they began their journey. The weapons were for the settlement, and no one had thought it likely they would be needed before reaching New Earth. Crichton could hardly believe he was considering this and based on what exactly? Some paranoid reports and some obvious infection? Surely they should be trying to contain it and help these people by finding a cure, instead of planning to fight and possibly kill them?

Crichton shook his head; the inner turmoil wasn't helping but he knew his instinct was right. In order to contain the situation they may have to use force. Then, maybe, Hallow could find a cure for those who hadn't gone too far.

'I'll open the armoury, but I think our first port of call should be gardening tools,'

162

Crichton said.

He placed his eye against the retinal reader and then his palm for further identification. As well as this, he had to key in a number to override any other passcodes. The greenhouse store opened and the guards went in, each quickly returning with machetes, shears and, of all things, a laser chainsaw.

Crichton went to the weapons store and followed the same procedure. Once inside they examined the guns and lasers.

'Too dangerous,' he said. But he took a pistol and a pack of bullets from one of the racks. The others followed suit. 'Only use these in absolute emergency and make sure you have time to aim properly.'

Before relocking the armoury, Crichton ran his hand over a cross-bow. The weapon was designed especially for the new world, in the event that the settlers didn't have power to run other weapons. Crichton took the bow and hung it from his belt as well as collecting a small machete from the gardening stores.

They loaded themselves up with more weapons, adding shears and a hoe to the pile which was now stacked onto a trolley to transport down to level seven.

'We'll pass these out when we get back to the others,' Crichton said.

'Crichton?' said Hallow. 'Look at this.'

Hallow was waiting in the corridor as the men loaded up. Crichton came to the door of

163

the store and followed his gaze. There were eight or nine men and women gathered near the greenhouse door.

'Where have you all been?' called Crichton, determined to maintain his commanding role among the crew. 'We've been looking for you.'

The group looked at him, heads turning like one person. The words *collective conscious* sprang into Crichton's mind but he didn't know where it came from. When they smiled, all in unison, Crichton couldn't stop himself from taking a step back.

'We've been searching for you,' said a voice.

The collective parted and Sasha and Gill stepped forward.

'They don't look sick,' said Hallow. 'They seem . . . different.'

'We aren't ill, Doctor,' said Gill. 'We are evolved. Your theory was right. We have successfully paired and now we are stronger than ever.'

Hallow felt something brush against his mind. A teasing sensation that frightened him because he began to suspect what it meant: they could read minds. He didn't question how they knew all about his theories. They had been watching somehow.

At that moment one of the women in the group convulsed and began to spit forth a torrent of worms. The creatures poured from her mouth and dissipated before they reached the floor.

'Some of you aren't,' said Hallow.

'We are not all compatible,' Sasha said. 'But in our new world we will need workforce.'

'What happens to them when they die? Why don't the worms keep feeding on them?' Hallow asked.

'We don't eat dead flesh, we live on blood,' said Gill.

Sasha raised her hand and Gill fell silent.

She's the queen, thought Crichton. *All insects have them.*

He began to walk forward and Hallow and the guards tentatively followed. But as he raised his machete the other people moved to block Sasha from sight. Gill, however, remained at the front of the group. He appeared to be directing them though he neither moved nor spoke.

'That doesn't explain it enough,' Crichton said.

The infected humans shuffled towards Crichton; their hungry mouths opening and closing. Some of them expelled the worms, and these all appeared to be in a state of rapid deterioration. They were little more than walking corpses and, as one of the guards had said, this was truly the stuff of nightmares and horror movies. Crichton recalled how Madison had beaten down Banks with only a fire extinguisher. He and the men had proper weapons now and he knew they could do this.

'Go for the head,' Hallow muttered as

though he could tell what was on Crichton's mind. 'The parasites are lodged in the cerebral cortex. That's how they control them.'

As the first of the creatures launched themselves towards him, Crichton swung the machete. He saw it pass through the air as though in slow motion, the nearest of the monsters raised his hand to protect his head. The blade sliced through, severing his hand and glanced off his shoulder. As Crichton heaved the weapon back, the arm of the man was cut off at the shoulder but he barely noticed it. Worms tumbled from the wound like maggots in a carrion, but the man, if he could still be called that, didn't stop. He hurled himself forward, falling on Crichton, teeth gnashing as he attempted to tear out his throat.

Another machete swung above the monster's head, burying in the top of its skull. Black blood exploded from its forehead and poured onto Crichton, he bucked and squirmed until the creature was pulled off him by one of the guards. Crichton swung the machete once more and lopped off the head of a female. He recognised her as one of the Bridge crew, but knew it was just too late for her. The lights were on but nobody was home. She wasn't human anymore. None of them were.

Gill fell on Hallow. He pulled the doctor towards him; his mouth open, and one of the

166

translucent worms squirmed on his tongue. Gill's mouth aimed for Hallow's, and even though he felt a strange compulsion to give in, the doctor turned his head away. He felt the worm wriggle against his cheek as the former engineer pressed his lips there. Then the thing disintegrated as oxygen reached it.

Crichton swung his blade, narrowly missing Hallow, and the machete bit into Gill's neck. He pulled back, ripping open Gill's neck and face. The skin dangled down over his jaw; Gill grinned. A sick laugh bubbled from his lips as he released Hallow and turned on Crichton. Gill ran his hand up over his face, pushing the ripped skin back into place. The wound began to close before the men's astonished eyes.

'That's impossible . . .' said Hallow as he staggered backwards against the door of the gardening store. He couldn't believe what he'd just seen with his own eyes.

One of the guards screamed. Two of the creatures had him and his machete fell to the ground as one of them bit viciously into his shoulder. The creature ripped back, teeth still buried in flesh and sinew. The guard screamed again and Hallow hurried to help, leaving Crichton alone to face Gill. Hallow charged at one of the creatures with a pair of garden shears which he opened and closed on the monster's neck. As he severed the head from the spine the thing began to die and fell into a further state of decay. Worms leaked from the wound then turned to dust. By this time, one of the other guards had killed another of the monsters and he hurried towards them and buried his now blood-soaked machete in the head of the creature that had bitten his colleague.

The wounded guard was soaked in his own blood but he raised his good hand and chopped his machete down on another of the creatures. This one was female and wearing the garb of the colonists. She hurled herself towards him, her jaws snapping hungrily at his bleeding shoulder. She fell at his feet with the first blow, and as his colleagues pushed back the other creatures, the guard rested against the wall, fingers clenched over the ragged injury, his body shaking with shock and fright.

Crichton, meanwhile, was circling Gill. The latter was smiling constantly. So confident was he that he couldn't be hurt.

'Where's Sasha gone?' yelled Hallow.

Gill's smile widened and Crichton began to think that they were all being kept busy while Sasha did something else but he could only speculate what that was.

'I've always respected you,' said Gill. 'Thought you were one of the good guys. I can make you like me.'

'Why would I want to be like you?' asked Crichton.

'You can't kill us,' Gill said. 'We are the future. You think humans are going to survive on a new planet without more resilience?'

'Gill, if there is anything of your former self left in there then you'll know that I won't join your new little club. I'm sworn to protect the colonists. I can't see how exposing them to some parasite is in their best interests.'

It doesn't matter what you think. You can't win.' Gill said.

Crichton swung the machete and Gill stepped agilely to the side. He moved his arm fast, backhanding Crichton, who fell back against the wall. Gill waited as Crichton pulled himself up: clearly he wanted the fight to last as long as possible. But Crichton wanted it over with, he was even more certain that these were some sort of stalling tactics. He swung the machete again, and once more Gill stepped away in the opposite direction. Crichton anticipated the move this time however and halfway through the swing he changed direction. Gill made no effort to protect himself. Surprise lit up his strangely normal features as the blade bit into his forehead, cleaving his skull like a ripe water melon. Gill's hands went up before him, opening and closing in a reflex gesture that was too little too late. Crichton threw his weight behind the blade. It was so sharp that it slid through Gill's face and jaw and came to rest in his neck, severing the spinal cord at the top of his spine. Gill's body crumbled, the grotesque shocked grimace still on his face.

Crichton pulled back on the machete, freeing it from the body with a wet slurp. There were no worms pouring from Gill: another sign that he and Sasha were very different entities from the zombie-like creatures the others had become. Even so, Gill was definitely finished.

'The head,' he shouted to the others. 'Sever the brain and they die.'

16

Attack

The glass lay on the floor, the water spilt out. Madison knelt to look closer at one of the translucent worms which was still wriggling in the liquid.

'What was in it?' Priddy asked.

'Look.'

Priddy knelt down as Tory came over with a cloth to wipe up the spillage.

'Wait!' said Madison.

'What is it?' Syra asked. She and several of the colonists had gathered around and were joined by Gershwin.

'There's something in the water, Gershwin,' Madison explained. 'I think it's some of those things that Banks was . . .'

Gershwin shook his head. 'You've imagined

it,' he said.

'Who else drank the water?' Madison asked.
'I almost . . .'

She remembered Gershwin passing her the glass. She looked at Tory. The girl appeared normal and on the surface, so did Gershwin, but Madison had been fooled before by Gill. Even so, she was certain Gershwin was different.

'I had some,' said Gershwin. 'I'm fine. In fact I feel pretty good, Water for everyone I think.'

Tory glanced at Gershwin and frowned. It gave Madison hope that she was okay.

'Tory? Did you drink yours?'

'I didn't have time, I was serving the food,' Tory said.

Gershwin took a step back into the crowd. 'What is wrong with you all? The water is fine.'

The translucent worm on the floor wriggled its way out of the small pool of water on the floor and turned to dust as the air reached it. Madison recalled her own drink and she stood, went back to the table where she left it and found it gone. It brought a whole new light on the survival of the creatures. They could clearly survive in fluid, but not when exposed to oxygen.

'Where's my glass?'

The crew and colonists looked around with confusion.

'You see, she's imagining things?' said

Gershwin.

'I saw it too,' said Priddy. 'There was one of those worms in the glass and if Madison hadn't seen it I would have . . .'

The colonists each began to examine their own drinks. Each group shrank away from the others in fear of contamination. Gershwin remained in the middle of the room.

'Tory . . .' he said. 'This is crazy. I didn't put anything in the drinks.'

'No one said you had, Carl. Madison was just questioning the water.'

'But I . . .' Gershwin began to tremble. His colour suddenly faded from a healthy hue to cold and grey. All the while his eyes darted in his head, from side to side, as though he were warding off an attack inside himself. He stumbled backwards. Three colonists nearest the bar cried out as he approached and they scattered like frightened birds being chased by a cat.

Gershwin staggered against the bar. He seemed to be holding himself up but when he turned back to look around the room a new cunning was in his eyes. It was as though Gershwin was no longer there and something else was.

'Carl . . .?' Tory took a step forward as Gershwin held out his hand to her.

Syra pulled Tory back.

'I want to help him,' Tory cried. 'We paired. Don't you understand?'

172

'It's not him anymore,' said Syra.

'We have to isolate him,' Madison said. 'He needs to be taken to quarantine.'

Priddy shook his head. 'Too late for that . . .'

Gershwin's body trembled. His posture became old and haggard and he staggered towards Tory with a new intent.

'Kiss,' he murmured. 'Just one kiss.'

Tory remembered the awful kiss that Banks had wanted to give, and the Captain's strange behaviour suddenly began to make sense.

'You're my girl now, Tory,' Gershwin said, and lunged for the girl.

Priddy pulled his large, blood-stained spanner from the deep pocket in his boiler suit and smacked Gershwin in the stomach. The man fell, but struggled to his hands and knees, still fixing Tory with a hungry leer.

'Get back Carl,' warned Priddy.

Gershwin laughed and then he began to crawl towards Tory like an excited puppy.

Priddy raised the spanner, and with a sickening crunch, connected it with his head. Gershwin still struggled, so Priddy hit him again and again, determined to stop him from reaching Tory.

When Gershwin stopped moving, Madison took the spanner from Priddy's hands. Priddy was breathing heavily, but was coming down from the attack. He looked at Tory who was standing, watching in shock. The girl was covered in splashes of blood and gore.

173

Syra grabbed a towel from the bar and passed it to Tory, helping her rub the worst of the splashes of blood from her hands and face. Then she threw it down over the remains of Gershwin's battered head. The body wasn't moving and everyone stood in stunned silence.

Tory turned in Syra's arms and cried against her shoulder. 'I can't believe this is happening.'

Eyes passed over the corpse, then back to Priddy, as they tried to make sense of what was happening.

'You killed him,' Lisbeth said after a minute or so. 'You're a murderer.'

'No,' said Madison, stepping forward to take control of the situation. 'There was something wrong with Gershwin. He was a danger to you. You could all see that.'

The silence was broken by the doors from the corridor crashed open, admitting Crichton and the others. They were shouting and terrified and it only took one glance at their dishevelled and blood-soaked state for Madison to realise that Crichton had been fighting his own battles. He was also fully kitted out with sharp weapons. The guards following him pushed a laden trolley into the centre of the room.

'Get those doors locked,' Crichton ordered. 'Anyone who feels able, pick up a weapon. There are more of these things on the way here!' Crichton said looking down at Gershwin's body.

174

Madison reached for a machete as the door opened again pushing aside the guard who had been trying to secure it. Sasha entered, followed by a shambling horde of infected crew and colonists.

There was a shared intake of breath from those in the Mess as they studied the newcomers. The colonists and crew were rapidly learning that something was seriously wrong. Some of them recognised friends and colleagues beside Sasha, but none were prepared for the blue-grey faced, ravenous monsters that they had turned into. It was difficult to comprehend but they had to accept it all and fight, or they would die.

Madison felt a momentary wooziness as she looked at Sasha. The girl was glowing again, as though she were projecting something from her body. Madison was reminded of an old film she had seen, where a witch changed her image to appear beautiful, but underneath she was a horrible, wizened crone. She tried to look beyond the shimmer but couldn't even though she realised that all around her the men and women were losing their urge to fight. The weapons were being slowly lowered, not raised. And people were starting to smile in a dazed manner.

'Goddamit! Snap out of it! She's doing this to you!'

Out of the corner of her eye, Madison saw Priddy move, he had fought Sasha before.

What was it he had said . . . he had focused on the alarm: the sound of the red alert. Madison threw herself away from the group. She had noticed an emergency button in the kitchen, near the door when Tory had held it open for her.

She forced her weakened legs to hurry towards the kitchen and as she reached it, the door opened and Ben Walsh was there. He looked like the walking dead. *That's what they are,* her mind screamed.

Behind her Madison heard screams and cries but didn't dare take her eyes off Walsh. She backed away as he walked towards her, arms outstretched. He smiled, and a torrent of vile worms fell from his mouth.

Someone touched Madison on the shoulder and she jumped. It was Syra. She too had grabbed a weapon, and had followed Madison back to the kitchen area.

Syra came alongside Madison and the two women faced Ben Walsh. Madison hefted her machete in her hand, and Syra raised her weapon: a small lasersaw.

As Syra started it up, the humming sound was enough to disrupt whatever influence Sasha had on the others and the sounds of battle erupted around her.

Walsh grinned manically.

'Let's open that smile up even more, Ben,' Syra said and as Walsh stumbled forward towards them like a confused Frankenstein monster, Syra swung the saw, and caught him under the chin. Walsh's jaw was severed in two and several of his teeth scattered like shrapnel across the room.

Madison didn't wait around to watch Syra finish the job. She slipped past Walsh and smashed the machete against the thin glass sheet that covered the alarm button. The alarm began to sound and Madison turned to see Syra impale Walsh through the stomach with the lasersaw. She lifted it up like a knife through butter, and Walsh's body fell, neatly cleaved in two.

Syra trembled, but smiled at Madison, and the two of them hurried back to the Mess. The noise from the alarm was drowning out the sounds of fighting. She pushed the door open and found that the crew and colonists were being cornered by the creatures. The more they killed, the more appeared from the corridor.

The Mess was bathed in blood.

Syra waded into the nearest infected colonist with the saw. Worms swarmed out of dismembered limbs, disintegrating as they hit the air. To her right, Madison saw Lisbeth fighting with her own partner. Lisbeth's eyes were crazed. She was trying to place her mouth over his, but he held her away, one hand around her neck. Eventually the man found a chair with his other hand, and smashed it down on Lisbeth. There was a loud crack and her body crumpled. Lisbeth didn't move again. Blood seeped out of the back of her head. Her skull was crushed, the creature inside her destroyed.

Meanwhile Crichton had cornered Sasha but she was too close for him to swing the machete he was holding. She was strong and, as they fought hand to hand, Sasha's lips never stopped smiling. It looked like a grimace though, and Crichton wondered if this was because the girl was in pain. He was also shocked by the way he had almost fallen under her spell. It became even more evident that earlier, when they were attacked outside the armoury, Sasha had been saving her strength for this final battle. She could have used it overpower them, but she hadn't. This could mean only one thing: her powers were limited. The thought gave Crichton hope and the courage to fight on.

'Shut the alarm off,' Sasha yelled and several of her creatures turned and began to leave the Mess. Crichton knew they would be heading for the mainframe computer room that housed the alarm system.

Meanwhile, Madison recognised one of her engineers amongst the horde and realised that he would know how to silence the noise. She ran up behind him and swung the machete. But she had so little strength left that the blade twisted in her hand and the blunt side glanced off the man's back. The engineer turned to look at her. She swung the implement again, this time using both hands to add strength and control. The blade hit home but she pulled back too soon. The engineer's neck was half-severed. Worm-infested blood leaked out and down his boiler suit. Madison felt nausea tugging at her. She didn't have the heart to see it through, but knew she had to kill him.

The maggot worms squirmed from the wound and as the engineer advanced, Madison lifted her arm and swung once more. The thought of this thing touching her was worse than the idea of killing him. Her blow hit home and the engineer collapsed at her feet, his head lolling from his neck. The horrible black blood pooled around his body and Madison turned just as another of the creatures reached for her.

*   *   *

Crichton was tiring. Sasha was too strong, far more so than Gill had been. He had wanted to capture her: he had thought that maybe Hallow could examine her and understand how this anomaly had happened. During the course of the battle two of the guards came between them. Sasha had ripped out their throats with barely a flick of her hand. Then, to his horror, Crichton had seen Sasha drink their blood and he knew then that she was just too dangerous to try to save. He was constantly reminded of the old horror movies from the twenty-first century. Vampires, zombies and monsters of all kinds were prevalent in those times. Deep down, Crichton had never understood the fascination, preferring to keep his feet firmly on the ground and had rarely indulged in fiction.

But these *things* were real. They were extra terrestrial—truly alien. How could they manipulate the minds of those they occupied? What were they anyway? Was it some fluke of bacteria that had somehow merged with human blood in order to create these awful things as Hallow had said? Or was this some truly alien life-cycle?

Around him the lesser creatures fought and struggled with the remaining colonists and crew. The pairings that hadn't taken was how Hallow had described them. Crichton wondered at how many there were, and how few had been successfully 'paired' from the parasite's perspective.

'You're right Crichton,' said Sasha as though she could read his mind. 'There are very few successes. This is because we need only a few of us to survive. The man you knew as Gill had become one with us. He had embraced us you see, but most of these others didn't. Their minds fought us until our larvae began to reproduce in an effort to bond. In the end, when they stopped fighting and finally melded, their human bodies had cannibalised

180

themselves beyond repair and their minds, bombarded by so many of our larvae, were ultimately of little use.'

Crichton backed away from Sasha, looking for a way to escape, and found himself beside Doctor Hallow, who had heard Sasha's explanation.

'Like selling your soul to the devil,' Hallow said.

They were joined by Madison and Syra, and the four of them faced Sasha.

'We don't accept you and we aren't making deals,' Syra said.

Syra swung the lasersaw, but Sasha was too fast. She ducked away, only to come face to face with Priddy.

His large spanner swung and connected with her skull, sending her flying backwards.

Hallow followed up and swung his machete, taking a chunk from her arm.

Seeing her stagger, Crichton saw his opportunity, and swung his machete in a hissing arc. Sasha, half fallen, was impaled, and shuddered as Crichton drove it home.

Madison became aware that the other creatures had turned away now from attacking the cornered colonists. Their queen was injured, and it would only be seconds before they would be fighting to save her.

'Kill her!' cried Priddy, hefting his spanner for another blow.

Syra swung the saw again. This time it bit

181

into Sasha's collarbone. Her chest was cleaved open as the laser teeth sliced through her. But still she struggled, her alien, inhuman eyes fixed on her attackers.

'The head,' said Hallow.

Sasha squirmed, trying to pull herself free. Madison and Priddy turned to face the oncoming horde.

This is it, thought Madison. *We are done for*. She turned back and raised her machete while Syra pulled back the saw. With a cry of defiance, Madison swung the weapon down on Sasha's neck.

The thing that was once Sasha screamed. It was an inhuman, wailing cry of pain and desperation, but it resonated with all of the colonists and crew. It sounded like the extinction of a race. The end of a populace. Madison felt a lump rise in her throat as the keening wail tailed off, and Sasha's head separated from her body.

As Sasha died, the other creatures staggered and halted their attacks as though they no longer had the drive to continue the fight. This allowed the crew and colonists to quickly finish them off. And, as one by one, they dropped lifelessly to the floor each fell into that extraordinary speeded-up decay process. As though the bodies were being held together by the worms and ichor and once the life-force was removed, so the creatures just disintegrated.

182

Madison, Syra, Priddy, Hallow, Tory and Crichton stood there breathing heavily. Some of the surviving colonists started to cry, while others comforted them.

'Hallow,' Crichton said. 'What the hell just happened here?'

'They were a collective mind. A bit like ants I suppose, except that their connection was so unique they couldn't survive without their leader. It weakened them. They lost direction and focus.'

Madison felt the shock reach her limbs and the blood-soaked machete fell from her fingers. She glanced at Crichton. They had won. But at what cost? Could they now all go back to their lives, heading for the future they had once believed in? Through gore-streaked eyes, Madison surveyed the devastation around her. It was difficult to see beyond the chaos. But she was strong and she would try to put this behind her. Humanity would survive to fight another day.